"This dance is already taken."

Using the same fierceness he'd used to make the street gangs of his youth back down, Cole glared at the man who would likely be his partner in the near future.

Rebelliousness set Bella's jaw, but Wong had already bowed out and turned away before she could protest. "Maybe I *wanted* to dance with Dr. Wong."

Most women would protest at Cole's high-handedness, and rightfully so. But tonight the caveman inside him wouldn't allow Dr. Wong to put his hands on Bella. Seeing her this afternoon had been such a shock. She had a career. She had a son. She had a life.

"Dance with me instead."

She glanced around, saw no easy way out, and agreed. No, she hadn't changed that much. The old Bella always did what society expected of her. Like marrying David Beautemps.

A wave of jealousy flooded through his veins. David had had a wonderful, intelligent and beautiful woman, and a son any man would be proud to call his own. They had seemed to be the perfect couple. What had gone wrong with their marriage? And why should it matter to him?

As he wrapped his arms around her Cole felt as if fragments of himself had fitted into place. There was a fullness, a wholeness about Bella pressed against his body.

He knew why he was dancing with her. Illogical though it was, he couldn't stand the sight of another man holding her—and he didn't feel like dredging up the strength of will to push away his baser tendencies. Not tonight. Not after all the turmoil his homecoming had stirred in him when all he'd wanted to do was bring comfort and cures to those who needed it the most.

But why did she clutch him equally as strongly?

Dear Reader

Think back on that one time in your life you wish you had said something—done something—differently. From that moment on your life took a different path.

If you could have a second chance to play out that moment again, would you take it?

Once a debutante whose life was filled with parties, single mother and Cognitive Behaviour Therapist Isabella Allante now devotes her time to providing a stable life for her autistic son. But, no matter how carefully she plans, she can't keep either her money or her energy from running low at the end of the month.

Specialist hand surgeon Dr Cole Lassiter, who was orphaned and raised by a charity, now gives most of his great wealth away. His life is steady and secure, but he can't buy what he wants most—a loving home.

How different would their lives have been if they had followed their hearts instead of their heads and got married after high school graduation? But they each made different choices and now they are both alone.

Cole and Bella get their second chance when their paths cross as they volunteer for the Special Games in New Orleans. Will they embrace their second chance or let this moment in time slip away?

I hope you enjoy reading about these two lovers that fate keep throwing together despite the world's attempts to keep them apart. Please let me know what you think of them and the decisions they make. Reach me at www.conniecox.com

Best wishes for health, wealth and happiness!

Connie

RETURN OF THE REBEL SURGEON

BY
CONNIE COX

First published in Great Britain 2012
by Mills & Boon, an imprint of Harlequin (UK) Limited.
Harlequin (UK) Limited, Eton House, 18-24 Paradise Road,
Richmond, Surrey TW9 1SR

© Connie Cox 2012

ISBN: 978 0 263 22886 1

Harlequin (UK) policy is to use papers that are natural, renewable and recyclable products and made from wood grown in sustainable forests. The logging and manufacturing process conform to the legal environmental regulations of the country of origin.

Printed and bound in Great Britain
by CPI Antony Rowe, Chippenham, Wiltshire

Connie Cox has loved Harlequin Mills and Boon® romances since she was a young teen. To be a Mills and Boon author now is a fantasy come to life. By training, Connie is an electrical engineer. Through her first job, working on nuclear scanners and other medical equipment, she saw a unique perspective into the medical world. She is fascinated by the inner strength of medical professionals, who must balance emotional compassion with stoic logic, and is honoured to showcase the passion of these dedicated professionals through her own passion of writing. Married to the boy next door, Connie is the proud mother of one terrific daughter and son-in-law and one precocious dachshund.

Connie would love to hear from you. Visit her website at: www.ConnieCox.com

**This is Connie's second book
for Mills & Boon® Medical™ Romance.**

Why not check out her fantastic debut?

THE BABY WHO SAVED DR CYNICAL

**Available in eBook format
from www.millsandboon.co.uk**

My admiration and gratitude goes out to all those
who care for both our physical and our mental health.
Special thanks to Kenneth Ashley, Phylis Caskey,
David Caskey, Keith Anderson and Kim Cox, who
share their medical knowledge and their healing hearts.

CHAPTER ONE

COLE had sworn he would never come back, but here he was, on the edge of his seat, watching the boy on the track who had never broken stride the whole five kilometers. He glanced at the second hand on his watch. The boy was doing a consistent six-minute mile.

The boy sprinted for the finish line, his ground-eating stride putting him ahead of the pack. Athletic grace like that could be honed by training but began in the womb.

Despite the New Orleans heat and humidity, Dr. Cole Lassiter kept his attention on the competitions as a way of keeping the painful memories at bay.

Today and tomorrow were track-and-field competitions at Tad Gormley Stadium in City Park. Thursday was the swim meet at the hosting hospital's full-size facilities and Friday was back at the track for the soccer matches. Then home to New York for the weekend if he could get loose ends tied up—or at least keep things from unraveling.

The wise thing to do would be to stay in New Orleans over the weekend to wine and dine the doctors and their families, and make sure everyone was comfortable with the merger of the two medical clinics.

If he could only keep his own personal unease from showing. His hometown of New Orleans held nothing but nightmares for him—and a lucrative possible partnership between

Lassiter Hand and Wrist Institute and the equally renowned New Orleans Sports Clinic. But negotiations were fragile.

A cheer from the bleachers had him turning his attention back to the field and the final lap of the race.

A modest but enthusiastic crowd encouraged the athletes as they competed for a sense of accomplishment as much as for a victory. These regional "special games" were hosted by a leading New Orleans hospital and run by scores of volunteers. It was certainly a different experience from the professional events he usually attended.

These games, free to all who wanted to watch, were every bit as exciting as the big-ticket events Cole usually went to. Maybe even more so, considering what these athletes were up against. All had mental challenges, and many of them had physical challenges, as well. But they had the same heart and courage as any other athlete.

From the sidelines, a distracted girl wandered onto the track right into the boy's path.

Cole winced as the boy jerked and hurdled to keep from running into her and ended up on his knees.

Without a word, the boy climbed back to his feet and took off running, trying to catch the two runners who had passed him.

He closed the gap to inches. If he'd had three more strides, he would have caught the front runner. Instead, the boy took second place.

An official leaned down to check the boy's knee, then pointed toward the medical tent. Without needing a prod from the intercom system, Cole headed in that direction.

From the moment she'd entered the stadium that morning, Bella Allante's attention had been drawn to him as if he had some preternatural power over her.

Why now? Why, when her world spun on the tip of a needle, did Cole Lassiter have to show up now?

Distracted, she tried to focus on the one-sided conversation her teenage helper was carrying on.

"So my mom says to tell you thanks. Working with our family photo album has really helped my sister understand age appropriateness much better."

"You're welcome." Isabella had stumbled upon her son's fascination with family photographs a few years back. "I've used them to teach everything from facial recognition to table manners."

"My sister is obsessed with photos of our grandmother. Didn't you tell us that happened with Adrian, too?"

"Yes, it did." Obsession wasn't an unusual trait for someone on the autistic spectrum. Isabella just wished Adrian's obsession had been with anyone other than Cole Lassiter.

The day her son had asked about the tall, dark-haired boy in many of her high-school photos, displaying curiosity but also being able to recognize him in photos at different ages, Isabella had been overjoyed at Adrian's breakthrough in development but torn about using the image of the man she despised above all others to teach her son.

Although she'd been mightily tempted to tell him a half-truth that day, she had never lied to Adrian. So she had confessed that the boy in the photos was Adrian's father, now a grown man and a renowned surgeon.

Instantly, she'd had to page through copies of her father's medical journals to show Adrian photos of Cole as an adult.

Since then, Adrian had elevated Cole to the status of superhero, insisting on having a dark-haired plastic doctor doll along with his superhero action figures and adding Cole's photo to the collection of pictures of family and friends on his bedside table.

She had been so thrilled she had found a way to reach her

emotionally locked-away son she had decided to encourage and embrace his fascination with Cole, in the certain belief that she would never have to deal with the man in person.

Was that Adrian in the lead? He never wanted her to watch him compete, so she had only seen him run from afar.

Once more she scanned the crowd, intently watching the athletes take their final lap.

What was Cole doing here—beyond watching the son he had never acknowledged? That small part of her that needed closure nagged at her now like it had so many dark nights in the past. Had she tried hard enough, done enough?

Isabella lifted her chin. An Allante didn't beg—and she would never stoop that low again. If only he had acknowledged her pregnancy in some way, she could have put her doubts behind her, along with those tarnished memories of first love.

"Ms. Allante, is something wrong?"

Isabella replaced her worried frown with a forced smile. "No—just anticipating a problem that might never happen."

If only it was just a commonplace problem worrying Isabella now, instead of the man in the front row, sitting all alone with his elbows propped on his knees.

The girl, old beyond her years, nodded with understanding. "My mom does that all the time. My dad keeps telling her to just take it each moment as it comes, but it doesn't seem to help."

Isabella tried to follow the same creed, even while she tried to provide an environment as secure and routine as possible for her son. While she was doing well on the secure environment part, she was failing miserably to live in the moment.

Usually her problem was trying to anticipate the future. But today her worry was all about the past.

Only fifteen short years ago, she had wished with all her heart to set eyes on Cole Lassiter.

She had wished it right up to the moment she had repeated her marriage vows to another man. At that point she had begun wishing just as fervently never to see Cole again.

Cole stood and stretched, spreading to the skies those arms that had once held her so tight, and began to amble toward the medical tent.

The loudspeaker popped and squealed, then blasted out, "Will the mother of athlete number 183 please meet him in the first-aid area?"

A burst of panic flipped her stomach with her heart. "That's Adrian."

"Go." The girl threw away the pencil Isabella had snapped in two. "I can take care of this."

"Thanks." Like she had every day since the pregnancy test had shown positive, Isabella straightened her spine, put her anxiety behind her, and vowed to do whatever was best for her child.

Under the tent in the makeshift first-aid station, Cole knelt to examine the boy's skinned knee.

"You're Adrian, right?" He was careful to move slowly and talk plainly.

"That's right, Doctor," an assistant answered for the boy. "Adrian is fourteen years old."

Cole would have guessed he was a year or two older. The boy was tall and rangy. He rocked back and forth as he flexed his left forefinger over and over again.

Adrian wasn't Cole's standard client. As a hand surgeon who specialized in sports medicine, Cole usually treated highly paid professional athletes.

He'd been informed that Adrian was autistic, mostly non-verbal, and skittish around strangers. Adrian particularly disliked being touched.

Volunteering for these special athletic games challenged

Cole's doctor-patient skills. He wasn't familiar with treating athletes with mental challenges, but he had stepped out of his comfort zone to fill in for one of the future partners who'd had a family emergency.

Family—something else Cole wasn't too familiar with.

Cole could relate to the boy, though. He himself was more of a thinker than a talker. Thankfully, professional athletes rarely required much chit-chat.

Still, he felt the need to be encouraging. "That was quite a race you ran, Adrian." Cole kept his voice calm and low despite the noise of the cheering crowd around them.

Adrian smiled with his eyes, showing acknowledgment of the compliment.

"Tough luck about the fall."

Adrian showed no anger, or even frustration, over the accident. Good sportsmanship personified.

"Adrian's mother is here, Dr. Lassiter," the assistant warned.

Before Cole could stand and turn around, Adrian's mother asked over his shoulder, "Honey, are you all right?"

He knew that voice.

Even after fifteen years, it rasped down his spine. Who would have thought a voice from his past could slam into his gut like this?

Calling on all the stoicism he'd developed over his career, Cole stood and moved aside so she could take his place. Isabella Allante was more beautiful now than the last time he'd seen her—sound asleep in his bed.

For the sake of the boy, Cole used every ounce of professionalism he had to reassure the anxious mother. "Adrian is fine. Just a scrape."

"Cole," Bella said in a monotone, as if she'd turned off a switch to her emotions. Her face registered nothing, a mask of calm.

She had always been good at keeping her emotions in check, a trait that would have made her a good doctor if she had gone to medical school as they had planned.

He did the math. Had marriage and pregnancy, not necessarily in that order, caused her to drop out? Had it been her choice or her husband's?

That husband should have been him.

Betrayal and anger made him turn away from her, even after all these years. No other woman had ever affected him this way. He'd hardened his heart to make sure of it.

Bella bent down to inspect Adrian's knee.

"Doesn't look too bad, huh?" she asked her son, the compassion switched on again.

Cole watched Adrian's face as his eyes shifted up and to the left, then back to his mother's mouth. Adrian's way of agreeing, Cole guessed, when Bella gave him a gentle smile.

Feature by feature, the boy didn't look much like his mother. His eyes were dark, almost black, while hers were a crystal shade of violet. His hair was dark, too. Thick and wavy compared to hers, straight and honey-blonde. At fourteen, he was at least three inches taller than his petite mother. Maybe it was his gestures or the way he held himself that looked so familiar.

Cole glanced at Bella's bare ring finger. Nobody had told him that her marriage had broken up—if, indeed, that was what her ring-free state meant. But, then, he'd made it clear to everyone back in New Orleans that he didn't want to hear the name Isabella Allante ever again.

"Worth the ribbon?" She held up a medal dangling on a red ribbon.

Again, Adrian spoke with his eyes, delight showing through their dark depths.

"Want to wear it?" She lifted the ribbon to place it around Adrian's neck.

His left hand started to pat the air while his shoulders tensed and his eyes took on a wild and startled cast.

Bella rocked back on her heels, giving her son space. "Okay, honey. Why don't I hold it for you?"

Adrian calmed and smiled, a sweet, pure smile like his mother's could be. "Momma."

Bella sucked in her breath. "Yes, honey. Momma. Thank you for that."

The loudspeaker crackled and the commentator announced refreshments for all the athletes and their guests. Adrian's eyes lit up. He pushed himself off his chair, not even wincing as he put weight on his injured leg.

Without looking left or right, he started for the snack bar. Abruptly, he stopped, pinned Cole with those deep, dark eyes and gestured, more a command than an invitation. Adrian might not use a plethora of words but his body language spoke volumes.

Cole could feel the tension radiate from Bella.

He had no problem reading her body language either. While Adrian clearly wanted Cole to accompany him, Isabella wanted exactly the opposite.

"Adrian, honey, Dr. Lassiter is busy. I don't think he can take a break with us," she said, making herself clear.

The odds were stacked against her. First off, Cole was thirsty. Secondly, Adrian wanted his company—and Cole sensed a specialness in that. And, thirdly, Bella had just issued a challenge Cole wouldn't walk away from.

"*Au contraire*, Mrs. Beautemps. I'm ready for a nice cold drink."

Cole had once lived or died by Bella's slightest desire, but now he wanted nothing more than to prove that what she did or didn't want had no influence on his decisions.

"It's Allante," she corrected.

"Divorce?" Not that it should matter. He wondered purely

out of curiosity. He'd always thought she and David Beautemps would stay together forever. But, then, he'd thought that about himself and Bella, too, until she'd dumped him.

"My decision," she clarified, as if that would mean anything to him.

He shrugged. "Not my concern."

"Then you shouldn't have asked."

Sorry. The flippant apology stuck in his throat.

"You're right," he forced out, swallowing down the bitter taste of concession.

He and Bella were ancient history—bad ancient history at that—and long since archived under "foolish youth." Any feelings between them should have been put to bed a long time ago.

Put to bed. Not the best metaphor to choose, not when he still remembered how that honey-gold hair spread across his pillow and down her trim, bare back all those years ago.

He took in her simple T-shirt dress, flattering but not new, and her wedge-heeled sandals that showed wear around the soles. Her simple clothes were very different from the fashions she'd once worn.

Fifteen years ago, her clothes had come straight off a Paris or New York runway. From the looks of things, she would have benefitted from a better lawyer, settlement-wise.

She brushed her hand down her dress then lifted her chin. "What are you doing here?"

"Business." The multimillion-dollar merger was the only thing that could have brought him back to his old hometown. Bella's father had been one of the founding partners of the sports clinic a few decades previously but Cole's lawyers had assured him that Dr. Allante had been out of the partnership for over a dozen years.

"You're not doing business at a track-and-field meet, are

you?" Her question dripped of disbelief with a tinge of suspicion.

Cole knew she had deliberately twisted his answer.

He couldn't have told her anything even if he'd wanted to. He'd done enough of these mergers to know how tenuous early negotiations could be. Confidentiality and secrecy played a big role in making these kinds of deals run smoothly.

But, then, he had no desire to tell her anything about himself or his life. They had nothing in common anymore but a painful past.

"As you can tell, I'm a volunteer for the special games' medical staff. I'm a last-minute substitute." Is that what he'd been to Bella? A substitute while David was away at college?

None of this mattered anymore, he reminded himself as he swallowed down a bitterness he'd thought was long gone.

At eighteen, he'd been sure he and Bella had a soul-deep connection, more than just teenage infatuation, but he'd been wrong.

Apparently, he'd been wrong about more than one thing. Cole had expected David Beautemps to provide Bella with the high-society lifestyle she'd always had. But people changed. He certainly had.

"What's up with David?" he asked, to prove—to himself as much as to her—that he didn't care.

Two years older than him, and almost three years older than Bella, David had been kind, gentle and generous, as well as wealthy. When Bella had chosen David over him, Cole had understood, on a rational level.

Still, he felt raw. He thought he'd extinguished that internal firestorm long ago, but seeing Bella seemed to have stirred up embers from the ashes.

"Daddy," Adrian said.

Next to him, Bella sucked in her breath.

Cole looked around for the man Bella had married, but didn't see anyone approaching them. Was she wary of her ex?

If so, David would have to come through him to get to Isabella or Adrian. Cole might not be a part of her life anymore, but he would never stand by and let a woman or innocent child be hurt. Especially not these two. Cole brushed that thought away. Any honorable man would do the same.

Adrian started to flap his hand in impatience.

"Adrian, the doctor is busy. He doesn't have time for a break with us." A breeze blew through, plastering Bella's dress against her, outlining her petite figure.

He couldn't stop himself from wanting Bella now just as strongly as he had wanted her on their last night together. Though now he understood that desire was purely a sexual response. Then, he'd wanted her enough to consider giving up his lifelong dream of becoming a doctor.

But dreams hadn't been enough for Isabella Allante. Not his dreams, anyway. Her own dreams of marrying sugarcane plantation heir David Beautemps and taking her privileged place in society had superseded his foolish plans for the two of them together, carving out their own unique niche in the world.

"I can take a break." Now he wanted to prove to her, and— he had to admit—to himself that she had absolutely no sway over him. "Lead on, Adrian. I'm with you all the way."

Maybe sitting across the table from her as if they were two old acquaintances with nothing more between them but a couple of sodas—and another man's son—would close a chapter of his life that should have ended a long time ago.

After this quick encounter, he would throw the book of his youth against the wall and get on with his life—as he'd thought he already had until their chance meeting today.

* * *

Isabella forced her shaky knees to carry her. She let her steps lag as she watched father and son walk in front of her. She needed time to think—time to breathe.

How could this happen? She had spent so many nights, so many years trying to resign herself to the loss of the only man she had ever loved. And here he showed up, made an immediate connection with his son and stepped back into her heart as if he'd never been gone from it. She had thought she'd locked him out of that sacred place for ever.

Pain radiated from her chest throughout her whole circulatory system. She felt as dizzy as if she had been whirled in a fast circle for the last fifteen years.

Stop it, Isabella. You don't have time for childish theatrics, she told herself. She used all her training as a cognitive behavior therapist to pull herself together. Taking note of her mental state and subsequent physical reactions, she exerted mind over matter to bring her heart rate under control.

Only through sheer willpower did she force her world to stop spinning. Now to evaluate the situation. She looked at the pair in front of her.

They both had that same easy, long-legged stride. Adrian's hair was a shade lighter but in time it would darken to that deep cocoa brown like Cole's.

Side by side, there could be no denying that Adrian was Cole's son. Adrian had that same olive complexion and would soon have the same heavy beard that Cole had at such an early age.

Bella had taken full advantage of Adrian's fascination with Cole in so many ways. Photos of him had convinced her son to swim, to eat his vegetables and, most recently, to shave.

She had always had a worry in the back of her mind. What would Adrian do on the off chance he ever met his father? Now that worry was a reality. But there were no fireworks, no meltdowns, no drama of any kind.

The only volatile reactions going on were inside her own heart.

Unpredictably, her son took meeting his father in his stride, accepting Cole as someone he'd known for years. And, in a way, he had.

Why was he here—and why now, fifteen years too late?

Why the cat-and-mouse game, as if he didn't know who Adrian was to him?

Was he assessing the extent of Adrian's autism before deciding on whether to claim him as his son or not? That seemed far too cold for the Cole she had once known. But, then, so had his abandonment of her all those years ago.

She had to face facts. A decade and a half ago she hadn't known Cole as well as she'd thought. And she certainly didn't know him now.

For the first time since Adrian's birth Isabella was glad he rarely talked. She felt bad about it, but she didn't wish it only for her own selfish purposes. She needed to find out what Cole's intentions were.

Maybe Cole would satisfy his curiosity and simply go away, and she could get back to the steady, stable routine that served Adrian so well. What would she do if he wanted to become involved in Adrian's life?

She might not be able to predict Cole's behavior, but she knew what she intended to do—what she had always done. She would protect her son at all costs.

Resolution made, she glared at the back of the man who had left her and never looked back all those years ago.

She'd tracked his meteoric rise in the medical community as a leading hand and wrist surgeon. How could she help it, being the daughter of a renowned surgeon herself? He now had institutes in major cities all over the U.S. to care for his high-profile clients.

His latest patient had been a promising child gymnast

with a wrist injury. Under his care she'd made a miraculous recovery. Rumors said the girl's mother had received Cole's personal attention as well—for a little while.

And there was her answer. Cole would be in and out of their lives so fast they would barely notice the blip. She just had to keep everything as smooth as possible for Adrian— and for herself.

Isabella caught up to them as Cole and Adrian stood before the counter. Quietly, she observed them, still not sure what she should do, what she should say in front of her son.

"Want a drink?" Cole asked, intently watching Adrian's face.

As Adrian looked down and to the right, Cole tried again. "Ice cream?"

Seeing a positive response, Cole narrowed the choices. "Vanilla? Chocolate? Whipped cream?"

While it took Adrian's new aides days to learn his subtle form of communication, it had taken Cole only minutes.

Of course he could communicate with his son. They were so much alike in so many ways. Cole had always been a man of few words—the ultimate strong, silent type.

And Adrian had spoken to him. Isabella waited weeks, sometimes months, for a single sound from her son. Cole had known him for only a few minutes and had already been gifted with one of Adrian's few words. *Daddy.*

Without turning around, Cole asked, "Bella, what would you like?"

You, Isabella thought before she could stop herself. "A diet drink, please."

Cole ordered for her while Isabella deliberately amended her thoughts. What did she want?

You, fifteen years ago.

Answers.

This day never to have happened.

But Isabella had learned a long time ago about wanting something, wanting someone. She couldn't always have her heart's desire just because she asked nicely. Cole had taught her that lesson well.

Isabella warred within herself. Her ingrained etiquette insisted she make small talk, but her protectiveness cautioned that an effort to communicate could be misconstrued as an effort to forge a bond.

They ate in silence. In the past, Isabella had been comfortable with Cole's contemplative moods. But today she knew he wasn't thinking. He was seething. Fire was in his eyes as he stole glances at her between bites. But why?

She was the one with the right to be angry. He had left her, accepting the scholarship for pre-med and, eventually, the residency at New York's Hospital for Special Surgery when she'd thought he would come back to New Orleans for her.

She'd been sold out for a ten-thousand-dollar grant. If Isabella had known that was how much money Cole could be bought for, she would have written the check from her own trust fund.

But, then, she hadn't known she'd needed to buy his love.

Adrian looked up at Cole, happiness shining in his eyes as he sat with his real-life hero in the flesh.

Cole returned the look, adding a smile and passing Adrian a napkin. Adrian took it from Cole's hand instead of insisting Cole lay the napkin on the table. That kind of trust usually took a carer weeks to establish.

The intercom blared, paging Dr. Lassiter to the first-aid tent. "I've got to go."

As he stood, a storm built in Adrian's face.

Please, not a meltdown. Not now. Isabella braced herself for the scene she would be dealing with the moment Cole walked away. At fourteen, Adrian's pubescent temper tantrums were becoming more and more difficult to deal with.

She began digging in her purse for Adrian's scarf, hoping the scrap of fabric would have a calming effect should Adrian's emotions overcome his learned behavior.

Cole turned to face Adrian, without doubt noting the mottled red in his face.

Would Cole judge her to be a bad mother? Many people would, if they had never had to cope with autism.

He looked Adrian in the eye, not flinching away as his son's whole body started to shake. While taking the scarf from Isabella and handing it to Adrian, he subtly put himself between her and her son. Did he realize his protective maneuver? Did he think she needed to be shielded from her own son?

Isabella herself prayed that day would never come.

Adrian twisted both hands in the scarf, his thumbs tracing the pile of the heavy cut velvet while he raised the satin side to his lips, taking deep breaths like they'd practiced.

Isabella held her own breath as she watched Cole.

If Cole showed any sign of belittlement or disdain for Adrian's self-soothing, it could set off Adrian's barely restrained emotions.

Cole gave Adrian a respectful nod. "Good job, Adrian. A man controls his temper around a woman."

He took a card from his wallet, scribbling on the back. "Here's my cellphone number, in case you ever need me." His glance took in both of them.

He put the card down within Adrian's reach then once again walked out of her life, leaving his empty promise behind.

CHAPTER TWO

COLE walked away, feeling Bella's eyes burn into his back.

Maybe he had overstepped the mark, giving Adrian his card. But an inexplicable compulsion deep within him had prevented him from cutting off his connection with the boy.

There was no connection—could never be a connection—between him and Isabella. She had severed that with a knife in the back.

The rest of the morning dragged by with only one other patient, a mother with a minor ankle sprain. While he tried to explain that four-inch heels and bleachers didn't mix, she attempted to seduce him with invitations for drinks on the veranda after her ex-husband picked up the children that evening.

She was exactly the kind of Southern belle he always imagined Bella would have turned into. Not that he thought of Bella often. He'd had to train himself quickly to put her out of his mind or he would have never made it through medical school.

But forgetting about her after seeing her today took all his mental prowess.

While he'd rather head to the hotel to put a heat pack on his aching neck, he headed toward the classrooms instead. He'd promised his office manager he would pick up some information on early recognition of learning difficulties. Her daughter's pediatrician was starting to suspect a problem. And heat packs wouldn't cure his problem anyway. Only time would heal a neck and shoulder strain—just like only time would heal his heartache. But how much time? Fifteen years should have been long enough.

He ducked into a full auditorium and leaned against the door frame. The man next to him handed over a sheaf of lecture notes that Cole took with a politely absent nod, intending to drop out as quickly as he dropped in.

That was when he noticed the speaker, Isabella Allante, at the podium. A video on a giant screen behind her showed Adrian in his younger years, staring into the camera, while other children enjoyed a birthday party.

"So you see, I understand. I'm one of you." She met the eyes of parents scattered around the room. "My son has autism and I can't cure him."

A frisson of emotion quivered through him, an emotion that was too big to name.

He had to look away from Adrian's stare.

Cole frowned and glanced at the paper he held then glanced at his watch. Wrong time zone. He was late for the workshop on early detection by an hour.

As unobtrusively as he could, he turned to leave. From the podium, Bella fell silent. Just a pause. Just a beat. Just enough to make everyone turn and look at him.

He'd never been one to be swayed by general consensus—unlike Bella. How had sweet, pliable Bella managed with a son as challenging as Adrian? Still, he chose to stay to keep from disrupting Bella's talk any further.

"I've learned to deal with the ups and downs of life with honesty about my strengths and weaknesses." She stumbled on her closing sentences before she found her rhythm again. "And honesty about my emotions."

If that was true, she'd certainly changed.

The ring of sincerity in her message kept the crowd enthralled. "As many of you know, my background is in cognitive behavior therapy. But my specialty is in pain management, not autism. Like you, I can't stay immersed in the study of my child's disability to the exclusion of all else. Also, like you, I want to do everything within my power to help my child live a contented and worthwhile life. And that includes taking care of myself, mentally, physically and spiritually, and asking for help when I need it. I encourage you to do the same."

Was Bella staring straight at him? How could she even see him through the crowd? He must be imagining her focus on him, imagining her eyes accusing him of—of what?

When Bella stepped down from the podium and a website address and phone number flashed on the video screen, replacing the birthday scene, Cole felt like he'd been given a reprieve.

Back when Cole had known her, Isabella had been the kind of girl who'd avoided confrontation at all costs. But she was no longer that insecure, unconfident girl she'd been. She rushed to catch Cole, almost running in her three-inch wedges, hoping her favorite shoes would hold together long enough to overtake his long-legged strides.

In the parking lot, he stopped next to a BMW with a rental sticker on the window and took a look behind him, pinning her with his stare. "You want to say something to me?"

Isabella glared right back. "Why are you here?"

She winced when her confrontational words came out soft and breathless. Her wispy tone had nothing to do with the flaring ferocity of emotion in Cole's eyes but was completely due to her being out of shape. She needed to start running with her son—if she could find a free slot in her schedule.

Cole gave her a once-over, a quick assessment from head

to toe. She resisted the impulse to smooth her hair behind her ear or cross her arms over her chest.

"I'm consulting on a few cases with the sports clinic."

"It's hard to imagine you working with the SC."

Cole had always wanted to work for charity, not for big money. In fact, he had been a bit of a reverse snob about money. He'd definitely gotten over that hang-up.

"It's hard to imagine you as the mother of a teenage boy."

She smirked. "Time does have a way of changing us— some of us for the better."

"You, Bella?"

"Definitely. And you?"

He lifted an eyebrow then redirected the conversation. "Where's Adrian?"

She had the petulant instinct to answer, *None of your business.* But she was more mature than that. Besides, wasn't it better to figure out his intentions instead of antagonizing him, so she could be prepared?

"At a boy-girl mixer."

Getting back on track, she asked, "How long will you be in town?"

"I'm not sure yet." He said it defensively, tensing his shoulders with a grimace.

His evasiveness set off warning signals. In her profession she had learned to trust her instincts and to read the unspoken message behind tone of voice and body language.

"You have changed, Cole. You were never unsure before. You were always so cocky and full of bravado."

"Bluffing my way through was the only way I could get where I needed to go. A poor boy on scholarship to one of the wealthiest college prep schools in the United States has to convince everyone—incuding himself—that he's good enough to be there." He stood incrementally taller. "I don't have to prove myself to anyone anymore."

Sadness swamped her. Sadness for what could have been. But Cole had chosen ambition over her and their child—when he could have had it all if he had stayed. "You never had to prove yourself to me."

"That's not how I saw it. You needed approval from your family and friends. Therefore, I needed their approval to be with you. You never even told your father we were dating, too afraid he'd forbid it if he found out."

"He would have, too, if David's mother had advised him to. And you know Mrs. Beautemps. She would have made sure we couldn't see each other."

Isabella loved her father with all her heart, but he had been totally overwhelmed at raising a teenage daughter after her mother had died, and had turned over all decisions, major or minor, to her mother's best friend, Marjorie Beautemps. Trying to honor her friend, David's mother had taken Isabella to her bosom, almost smothering her, until the divorce.

Even though Mrs. Beautemps' hostile rejection hurt, Isabella could now draw a full breath without being reminded of society's proprieties.

Where would she and Cole be now if she had been a rebellious wild child instead of a submissive and insecure teenager? Of course, getting pregnant with Adrian could have gone a long way toward eroding her good-girl image if David hadn't married her, letting the world assume Adrian was his child.

But Cole wasn't part of that world. She'd done everything in her power to let him know the truth and he had chosen to ignore it. She searched his eyes for a sign, a flicker of guilt or remorse. All she saw was cold, hard pride.

Cole gave Isabella a tight smile. "What we were, what we might have been—that's all in the past, isn't it? Anything between us is best forgiven and forgotten."

Isabella thought of her beautiful son as Cole shrugged off

their past together. How could Cole dismiss Adrian so easily? He had seemed genuinely interested in their son earlier. Something wasn't adding up.

What about the letter written in his scrawled handwriting that was locked away in her jewelry chest? For the first time since she'd ripped open that envelope, a niggling of doubt wormed its way into her thoughts. There was no way he couldn't know—was there?

"Cole, maybe we need to talk." Her phone vibrated a warning alarm, reminding her it was time to pick up Adrian. "But not now."

He gave her a hard frown that finally softened around the edges. "Anytime, Bella. For old times' sake."

It was the last day of the games. It seemed they'd gone on for four years instead of four days. Isabella was exhausted. She wanted to rub her eyes with the back of her hand, but smeared mascara wouldn't make the fashion statement she was going for.

To say her nerves were frayed was like saying the Titanic had hit an ice cube. This morning she felt like she was going under just as fast and fatefully as that famous ship.

All because of Cole Lassiter.

She'd been waking up in the middle of the night, going over and over in her mind those weeks she had spent trying to get a response from Cole.

Cole had to know about Adrian, right? After all she had done to inform him, how could he not know? How could he act so unparent-like toward Adrian? But, then, it took more than sperm to be a father, didn't it?

At her side, Adrian's hand rhythmically beat the air. Such big movements only happened when his world was off-kilter.

Her son was picking up on her mood. Out of the blue, he'd decided he didn't want to brush his teeth this morning.

Heaven help her, she'd resorted to her old method of persuasion and told him that his father always brushed his teeth so he wouldn't have stinky breath and people would like him. That had promptly taken care of the problem.

It had also set her to wondering what woman got to take advantage of Cole's minty-fresh breath nowadays—even while she castigated herself for caring.

She took a look around the field where the coaches organized their teams while waiting for the start of today's activities. Since Adrian didn't play soccer, he would have to stay by her side while she took care of her volunteer duties.

For the past few days Isabella had invoked all her willpower to give Adrian the privilege of wandering the grounds within her eyesight instead of making him stick with her. She was trying her best to let him have more independence, but was having a hard time letting go.

But today had nothing to do with independence but with mother's intuition. She could tell by the rebellious glint in his eye that she couldn't trust him to stay out of trouble by himself.

"Hi," drawled a deep Southern male voice behind them.

Isabella's heart skipped a beat until her head caught up with her and she realized it wasn't Cole.

The man was the father of one of Adrian's friends.

Why was she jumping every time she heard a man speak? She'd been doing that every day since her first encounter with Cole, and not once had he approached her.

Just because today was the last day of the games, did she think he would seek her out to say goodbye? Not likely.

"Could Adrian hang out with us today? My wife is helping on the field and we could use the company."

"Sure." She watched as the two boys raced each other up into the stands safely under proper supervision. The resourceful father produced two pair of cheap binoculars from his bag.

Adrian held a pair of binoculars up to his eyes and scanned the field, looking for his own father, his hero come to life.

Because she couldn't stop herself, Bella took a look toward the medical tent with little expectation of finding Cole there.

Everyone took pride in the special games being conducted as safely as possible and this week's regional competitions were no exception. Which left a doctor with too much time on his hands. Apparently, sitting in a stifling medical tent while awaiting a medical incident wasn't Cole's style.

For the last several days he'd been everywhere, helping out at the registration table, chaperoning the non-competitive activities and handing out medals, which pleased her athletic son beyond imagining as Cole presented him with a slew of blue, red and green ribbons for his various competitions.

Everywhere Cole could be found, there was Adrian. And all that time Cole had said nothing, done nothing, to acknowledge Adrian as his son.

He'd seemed to be avoiding her, too. Not that she had sought him out. She didn't have to. That same awareness of each other they'd shared all those years ago gave her a sixth sense in knowing where he was the whole time he was on the stadium grounds.

What was his game? That was the thought that had been uppermost in her mind the past four days.

She had reverted, she was ashamed to admit, back to that passive girl who waited for answers to come to her.

Well, she had waited long enough.

Today she would make him listen. She would look him in the eye to make sure there was no misunderstanding and tell him he was too late. Neither she nor Adrian wanted him in their lives…

But Adrian *did* want his father in his life.

She stumbled over a lost pompom, almost losing her balance.

Still, she needed to protect her son from the emotional highs and lows of his father dropping in once every fourteen years or so. Adrian didn't handle upsets well. Better to keep Cole as a fantasy superhero than a flesh-and-blood man.

Was she doing the right thing for Adrian? That was what it all came down to.

Taking a deep breath, she started the long walk toward the medical tent.

Once there, she asked the volunteer, "Have you seen…?" Why was it so hard to say his name? "Dr. Lassiter?"

The white-haired grandmother working the desk gave her a quick shake of the head. "Not today. He's a busy one, isn't he?" She gave Isabella a wink. "And handsome, too. If I were a few years younger, I'd be looking for him myself."

"You'd have to stand in line," the nurse on duty added. "In fact, I'm old enough to be his—ahem—older sister and I would catch a drink or supper with him if he asked. He's as nice as he is beautiful."

Isabella shoved down the absurd possessiveness that welled up in her. History proved that even when he had vowed undying love, Cole had never been hers to keep.

"When Dr. Lassiter shows up, could you page me?" Isabella felt like an overaged groupie as the two women raised their eyebrows at her. "It's important," she added. Even to her own ears, she sounded like a desperate woman pathetically trying to attract the attention of a rich, handsome doctor.

"Aren't you Isabella Allante? Dr. Allante's daughter?" the nurse asked.

Isabella nodded. "Yes, I am."

"I worked for him right before he retired."

"I'm sorry. I don't remember…"

"Understandable. You were busy getting married and having babies."

"Baby. Just one."

"A boy, right? Your father was always talking about his grandson. He was so proud. Dr. Allante was a brilliant doctor and a pleasure to work for. Please give him my regards."

"I will. He still keeps up with the progress in his field." The subscriptions to his favorite medical journals and newsletters cost her dearly but they fed her father's mind and spirit even though the stroke had taken away his mobility. And they gave her a chance to keep tabs on Cole—for Adrian's sake, of course.

"I'm afraid you've missed out on seeing Dr. Lassiter. I still work for the sports clinic as Dr. Wong's office nurse. Since Dr. Wong will be in surgery all day with Dr. Lassiter, he asked if I would mind working the medical tent at the games today. I understood that Dr. Lassiter was headed back to New York after that." The nurse gave her a lighthearted grin. "A lot of us are wishing he would stay a little longer. He certainly adds something to the scenery."

Isabella had the strongest urge to tell the nurse that Cole was more than just another pretty face. Instead, she clamped down on her own confused feelings, a mixture of relief and disappointment.

The relief came from avoiding a confrontation. No matter how direct she learned to be, she still didn't like confrontation.

The disappointment, she told herself, was because Cole's departure left unfinished business between them. He didn't owe her a goodbye, although he certainly owed Adrian that and a lot more.

"Thanks for letting me know." Did that mean he'd left without saying goodbye to his son?

Isabella tried to suppress the thought that kept popping up over and over again. Somehow, by some weird twist of fate, could it be possible Cole didn't know Adrian was his son?

As she headed back to her volunteer post, she shrugged

away that crazy notion, just like she'd shrugged it away a thousand times in the last few days.

How many messages had she left on his voicemail all those years ago? For days and weeks she'd called, trying to reach him over and over again at all hours, hoping he'd pick up the phone so she could say what she needed to say in person. She'd written to him every day until a week before the wedding, hoping the deluge of mail would break through the barrier David's mother had built between them.

She'd thought that if she could only make him listen, she could explain that the engagement announcement to David had been none of her doing. That she had no intention of marrying anyone but him. That she carried his child.

But the letter she sent, the one she'd poured her heart into that he'd returned in pieces, had said it all.

Anger at Cole, confusion about what to do next and relief that Cole was gone and life would eventually get back to normal warred within her, making her stomach roil.

Isabella evaluated. The only action she had to take was to tell her son his father had returned to New York.

It was a discussion she dreaded more than any other conversation she'd had in her life.

Cole walked into the doctors' lounge, soaking in the atmosphere he thrived on. The E.R. doctor snored on the couch in front of a muted television. Two other doctors consulted quietly at a side table over cups of coffee.

Successful surgeries always sent Cole Lassiter's spirits on a soaring high.

Still, it didn't replace the lift Cole had gotten used to for the last few days whenever he'd seen that sweet, shy smile of Bella's son. How could a kid worm his way into his heart so fast? Was it a pseudo-affection for what might have been?

That boy should have been his.

"Glad to have you on board, Dr. Lassiter." One of the radiologists greeted him. Cole recognized him as a radiologist contracted with the sports clinic.

"Thanks." He held out his hand to shake. "Call me Cole."

He wanted to explain that he wasn't staying. He had applied for and received hospital privileges as a matter of course since that was where the sports clinic mainly practiced. But negotiations were too tenuous.

That was the excuse he gave his office administrator when he told her he needed to stay over the weekend. That was the excuse he gave himself in the light of day.

But last night, as he'd lain in his bed, he had dreamed of Bella and woken up heavily sad when he'd realized it had only been a dream.

He needed closure and he now had a few extra days in New Orleans to find it.

He sent silent thanks to his excellent office manager, who was shuffling schedules so he could steal this time for himself, a rarity in his hectic calendar.

Walking over to the kitchenette, Cole spread out his lunch of oyster po'boy sandwich and sweet iced tea, a New Orleans specialty.

"Mind if I share this table?" the radiologist asked.

"Not at all. I would enjoy the company." And the distraction. Normally, after a complex surgery like the one he had just finished, all he could think about was the details of the procedure and the next step to recovery.

Today, he thought about her.

Cole picked up his sandwich and took a bite, letting the flavors roll around on his tongue. Yes, it was as good as he remembered—proof that New Orleans wasn't all bad for him. He hoped this good feeling carried over into his partnership talks.

After that morning's surgery, he was more convinced than

ever that merging his institute with the sports clinic was the right thing to do—even if the practice had originally been built by Dr. Allante.

Who would have ever thought he wanted a relationship with anything that had to do with an Allante?

What role had Bella's father played in their break-up? Once he had gotten over the immediate pain, he had been grateful to David's mother for sending him that engagement notice. Just when had Bella intended to tell him about David? Would Bella have continued to play him the whole time she'd been planning her nuptials with the Beautemps heir?

Thinking of Bella made his stomach churn. Even the delicious sandwich lost its appeal.

"Filling, isn't it?" the radiologist asked as he took his last bite.

Cole stared at the half-eaten meal before him. "Yes, it's certainly a full plate. Much more than I want."

What an analogy for all the emotional trauma seeing Bella was causing him. All the stirring up of old hurt was much more than he wanted, much more than he had expected.

"So how did a New Orleans boy end up going to college in New York? We've got so many great medical schools here."

"I got a scholarship." But he'd had local scholarships, too. "I wanted to get away."

He'd never been further north than the Louisiana state line. Going to the big city of New York had seemed like a grand adventure. He had taken it for granted that Bella would wait for him.

The engagement announcement had come at the worst possible time. He'd been having a tough time adjusting to the rapid pace of New York after the slower pace of New Orleans. The accelerated undergraduate program he had thrown himself into required keen focus to stay caught up, let alone to excel.

"I'd like to see New York, but the wife always wants to go the beach on our vacations."

"Hmm." Cole gave a noncommittal grunt.

The radiologist took the hint and ate the rest of his meal in silence.

Cole turned his attention back to his meal but couldn't turn his thoughts away from Bella.

Bella had always seemed content to Cole. That was one of the qualities he'd liked best about her, always willing to go along with whatever he'd wanted to do. But, then, he hadn't been that special after all. She had gone along with whatever anyone had wanted her to do.

He had been at school a few short weeks when he'd received the newspaper clipping with Bella's beautiful smile in black and white along with the announcement of her marriage to David. The notice had included details of both their pedigrees and social standings, and it had been the only answer Cole had needed as to why she had chosen David over him.

The thick French bread of his sandwich sat too heavily in his stomach and the highly seasoned Cajun fries tasted flat and cold.

He'd made the official break-up as quick and painless as possible, a fast call that had gone directly to her voicemail—the fact that he hadn't had to speak to her in person had been his only break. That should have been the end of it.

But then she had started in. Call after call. Letter after letter. How many times had she called him? Hundreds?

They had all finally stopped after he'd written his own letter, making it perfectly clear there could be nothing between them anymore.

He took a sip of his sweet tea, trying to rinse the bitterness from his attitude.

He had deliberately got drunk on Bella's wedding day—for the first and only time in his life. For his own sanity as much as for the sake of his grades, he'd exerted great will-power and erased each call, destroyed each letter, before re-living the betrayal over and over again.

Instead, he'd thrown himself into his studies, the one thing he could always count on in his life to distract him from his grief.

Cole gathered up the remains of his meal and threw it in the trash.

Nothing about Bella should matter to him. How could he make himself stop wanting her? Why, after fifteen years, was he still asking himself that question? It was about time he found an answer.

Cole stretched, trying to stop the dull throbbing in his left shoulder that traveled down his arm to his fingertips—the results of tensing during surgery.

"Long surgeries will cramp you up, won't they?"

"Yes, they will. Occupational hazard." Only the surgery hadn't taken that long, a mere hour and a half compared to the five and six hours of reconstructive surgery Cole was used to performing. And he'd been a consultant while Dr. Wong had done most of the work.

He flexed his numb fingers.

Strained shoulder muscles took a while to right themselves. He'd give it a few more weeks before he had it checked out. Of course, that was what he'd told himself a few weeks ago. Maybe he should schedule a therapeutic massage soon.

Some pain-management specialists studied massage, didn't they? He reined in that runaway thought. It didn't really matter what Bella had studied, did it?

The natural high Cole felt after that morning's successful surgery was starting to fade, replaced by a need he wanted to deny.

Bella.

After only a few short days he had become addicted to that jolt of energy the sight of her gave him.

Neither of them fit with his old memories of a more pubescent, hormonal time. She had changed even more than he had. Why did it matter to him? How could he make it stop mattering?

CHAPTER THREE

AFTER a long, leisurely swim and a nice parboil in the whirl-pool, Cole checked his messages before making rounds.

His office manager had made sure his tuxedo was delivered to his hotel room for that night's special games reception.

He could tell himself he was staying to firm up the partnership, but in reality today's observance of Dr. Wong in surgery had put all his fears to rest. The lawyers could now go forward without further input from him.

Bella. *His own personal temptress.* But he was no longer that insecure boy hiding behind bravado. That was what he had to prove to himself. That was why he'd changed his plans. That was why he'd stayed.

He donned his best bedside manner and pushed open the door.

Without a greeting, his patient, Heath Braden, confronted him. "Tell me the truth, Doc. What are my chances of regaining full use of my hand?"

Heath no longer had the grip of a fireman.

Cole made himself look into Heath's eyes. "Slim. You will be able to do tasks that don't require as much strength or dexterity as you've had in the past, but passing the assessment tests to get back to active duty may not be possible."

Cole inwardly winced at the fear crossing the young man's face. He'd seen it time after time—would his loved ones still love him if he wasn't the man he used to be? Sadly, too often the answer was no, but Heath wasn't a highly paid athlete with a high-maintenance spouse.

Heath's wife leaned down to kiss her husband's forehead. "I don't love you for your hand. I love you for your heart."

The emotion between the two made Cole feel superfluous. He excused himself and headed to the nurses' station.

Heath's nurse gave him a rundown of the report. "Mr. Braden's condition could be easier on him but he doesn't want to take his pain meds, Dr. Lassiter. He says he doesn't want his son to see him all drugged up. He wants to be able to focus enough to enjoy his son's visits."

Cole understood completely. "The pain meds are for his comfort. Taking them won't affect the surgery or his recovery as long as he keeps taking the anti-inflammatories. But he will be in quite a bit of pain when he starts his physical therapy rehab. Do we have anyone who could do pain-management counseling with him?"

The nurse nodded. "We have a great therapist on staff who works wonders with biofeedback and hypnotherapy. Her schedule is always booked with a waiting list, though."

Having enough personnel to go around was always an issue, especially in a teaching-charity hospital like this one.

"Surely she could be convinced to add one more patient to her list. Give me her name and number and I'll have my staff set up an appointment for Mr. Braden."

"I'm glad to hear you're open to cognitive behavior therapy, Dr. Lassiter," the nurse said as she scrolled through the contact list. "Not everyone is willing to give CBT a chance. But we've seen great results as long as the patient trusts and believes in the therapy."

"I'm open to whatever works."

The nurse handed him Bella's contact information on a slip of paper. If Cole had been a fanciful man, he might believe fate was playing tricks on him to throw Bella his way. But it all added up. The hospital sponsored the games and Bella had volunteered, just as he had, to be part of that sponsorship.

Of course, with Adrian, she had a vested interest in the special games. So it was rational, almost inevitable, they would end up in the same medical circles.

The odds of their ending up in the same circle all those years ago had been much higher. And he'd been on the outside perimeter while Bella had been at the center of it all.

He made a quick call to his office manager, giving her Bella's contact information.

"Monday morning. Make it happen," he instructed his office manager.

"Yes, Dr. Lassiter. I will."

He surrounded himself with competent staff, so he could confidently put this problem out of his mind and focus on what was important. But, then, he'd been trying to put Bella Allante out of his mind for the last fifteen years and hadn't succeeded yet.

As Cole tucked the note in his pocket and turned away, a sharp pain arced through his neck and down his arm. He could use some pain management himself. Could Bella help him work through his pain?

There had to be a high level of trust between a medical professional and a patient, especially with the kind of work Bella did. No, with what they had between them, Bella couldn't help him. Not if he needed to trust her first.

Isabella's hands ached from gripping the steering wheel of her sensible fourteen-year-old car too tightly. Consciously, she relaxed, head to toe. Stress would only eat up the little energy she had left after such a long week.

Pulling into the hotel's parking lot, Isabella pasted on her social smile and summoned up her last smidgeon of energy, hoping it would be enough to get her through the special games recognition and fundraising event.

If she could find reserves for just a few more hours, she could go home and collapse for the rest of the evening. She might even be tired enough to sleep through her worries about Cole and the paternity discussion they needed to have. Or did they, since he had now gone back to New York, where he belonged?

Starting now, she would forget about this week and go back to providing a safe and predictable world for her son. If life was too predictable for her at times, that was one of the sacrifices of motherhood she willingly accepted for her son's well-being.

When she'd left Adrian in David's care, he had been fingering his scarf while hugging the framed photo of Cole that usually sat on his bedside nightstand, all the while keeping a steady pace in the gliding rocker next to her bed. His favorite video played so quietly on the television she could barely hear it. His plastic doctor action figure lay next to the television control within easy reach.

She'd been worried about overstimulation from the active weekend so different from their normal routine. And that had just been from participating in the local games. With Cole on the scene, she would have expected Adrian's reactions to be all over the board.

Instead, Adrian was taking the appearance of his father in his stride while she was struggling to contain her own anxieties.

Take a step back, Bella, she told herself.

She might be borrowing trouble. Cole might have made his once-in-a-lifetime appearance and now be gone for ever and her life could get back to the way she'd organized it.

Illogically, on top of the anger, confusion and relief, that idea made her very sad.

She had explained Cole's absence to Adrian by telling him Daddy had to work. It was the total truth, and Adrian had understood. Tomorrow, when both she and Adrian were better rested, she would break the news that Cole had gone back to New York.

She wasn't looking forward to tomorrow.

As she had so often since Adrian's birth, she vowed to live one moment at a time and let the future work itself out—but it was such a hard thing to do for a planner like her.

Tonight Isabella's job was to work the room, making a subtle plea for donations of time and money to support their local special games, a program her family had always championed before they'd ever had an athlete of their own participating. She recognized most of the faces in the crowd from her inner circle—or what had been her inner circle—as well as from the volunteers who gave so much of their time to make this program work.

Normally she could call up her inner sparkle and zest on demand, but Cole had knocked her off her game.

She smoothed the vintage wool skirt she'd inherited from her mother's collection of expensive and well-preserved clothing and wished she hadn't gone with an upswept French twist. Her bare neck made her feel exposed and vulnerable.

From the podium, the local chairperson was giving his standard speech, against a backdrop of happy athletes on a screen behind him. "Three and a half million athletes will train and participate in local games like ours on a state, national and global level. None of this is possible without dedicated volunteers and generous donors."

While there was no more Allante money to give, Isabella did what she could. One thing she'd been taught from birth had been the social graces that made working a room one of her greatest talents. She just needed to put Cole from her mind, pull herself together and get on with it.

She looked for those not with partners. Group mentality being what it was, a single mixing into a circle of couples took more charm than she had energy to give at the moment.

Being single usually didn't bother her—or rather she'd been able to bury all her disappointments and regrets. How could she look at her beautiful son and wish her life had been different?

But there were times like tonight, being single in a world of couples, when she felt incredibly, soul-searingly lonely.

She often had to go days, maybe even a full week, without human touch. Although she advised others to make friends with affectionate people, friendships took an investment of time to nurture. If anyone were to accuse her of not being the best at taking her own advice, that person would be right.

Lately, she'd been incredibly busy with her practice. Any time and energy leftover had gone into helping to organize this weekend's games and fundraiser. Then there had been all the mental work with Adrian so he could ready himself to step outside his routine comfort zone and participate in the games. She could only be stretched so thin.

Thus was the life of a single parent of an autistic child.

But, being a therapist, Isabella knew there was no such thing as a "normal" life. She glanced over at Darla with her practiced expressions of frivolity. One outwardly perfect husband with straight white teeth, a politician's smile—and a mistress stashed in an apartment downtown that they all pretended didn't exist.

Then there was Corrine, with her two beautiful, over-achieving daughters, one in rehab and the other fighting bulimia. Corrine, herself dangerously close to being addicted to pain meds, came into her office twice a month, trying to master drug-free ways to control her migraines.

In her private practice catering to the rich and powerful of New Orleans, Isabella knew many of these people's secrets—

which only positioned her even more squarely on the outside, looking in. She was only able to discuss the most banal of topics lest she reveal confidential information. Always on guard, keeping secrets so that everyone appeared perfect on the outside.

But, then, she'd been trained for pretending to be perfect her whole life. Perfectly poised. Perfectly in control. Perfectly satisfied with her solitary life.

David's mother had made sure she'd learned those lessons when she'd become Isabella's mother figure after her own mother had died—except for the solitary life one, of course. The plan had been to marry Isabella to her son. It had been a good plan for a while.

What would her life have been like if her fun-loving mother had conquered the breast cancer that had slowly taken her life?

With all her practice, Isabella should be perfect at not looking back and asking what if? Some nights were easier than others.

She glanced around the room. Perfect couples made up of perfect women and perfect men—at least on the surface.

It would take a bona fide perfect man to want her. A man who saw beneath the surface and accepted her and her son, imperfections included.

No chance of finding that perfect man here tonight.

"Thank you to all our volunteers. There would be no games without you. See how you've enriched lives," the local chairman began, as he gestured to the screen showing the athletes with expressions of determination, victory and joy.

As the chairman continued thanking benefactors and volunteers, Isabella let herself get caught up in the images of the athletes, their coaches and parents. This one hundred percent volunteer organization had given both her and Adrian such support and growth. She was proud to be a part of it.

"...thank Dr. Cole Lassiter for being our attending physician on-site. We had need to call on Dr. Lassiter at the last moment, and he rescheduled his own personal plans to answer our call. Excellent job, Dr. Lassiter," the chairman said as he initiated applause.

Isabella's stomach lurched when she heard Cole's name.

He shouldn't be here, not in her carefully constructed environment. He should be on his way back to New York.

This was her world. Not his.

All the questions Isabella had been trying to bury deep in her subconscious bombarded her mind, making her head hurt.

One thing was for sure, a gala event was not an appropriate setting to discuss relationship issues and complications. Right now she had a party to get through. One moment at a time.

She tamped all those conflicting emotions down deep and put on her brightest smile. Discreetly, she stood on tiptoe to catch sight of the illustrious wonder surgeon, but she couldn't spot that wavy black hair across the crowded ballroom.

Instead, she found herself elbow to elbow with Dr. Lockhart, one of the sports clinic's original partners. By his side was his daughter Madelaine. Isabella had gone to school with Madelaine since kindergarten, where they had disliked each other on first sight.

Dr. Lockhart spotted her first. "Isabella, so good to see you. Do you know Dr. Wong? We've recently begun to expand and he's our newest partner."

Isabella held out her hand. "I don't believe we've met. Thank you for coming tonight to support the games, Dr. Wong."

"It's just Wong. That's what all my friends call me." Dr. Wong took her hand. "It's my pleasure. I noticed you when you arrived this evening. If I'm not being too forward, perhaps we could dance later."

He had noticed her? It felt good to be attractive to the opposite sex. The way Wong held on to her hand a little longer than normal flattered her needy ego. If only she felt the same prickles of awareness Cole had raised in her.

For some irrational reason, knowing Cole could be lurking nearby made Isabella feel like she was being disloyal by even thinking such a thing. It was becoming clearer and clearer that she had some issues to work through—and not only those related to her son.

To counteract her misplaced feelings of guilt, she gave Wong her most flirtatious glance. "I would like that."

"Isabella's father was one of the founders of the sports clinic," Dr. Lockhart told Dr. Wong.

"I remember seeing his name on the plaque in the office waiting room. I understand your father is retired. I would like to meet him. Is he here tonight?" Wong had a nice, easy smile.

"He had a stroke about twelve years ago." That had been when Isabella had found out about her father's debt-riddled estate that had become her inheritance and her responsibility.

While she loved her father dearly, his sole passion had been medicine. Anything else, like money or child-rearing, he had gladly relinquished to someone else. At least Mrs. Beautemps had been more scrupulous when overseeing Isabella than her father's accountant had been when overseeing his finances. Or at least most people would think so.

Since the divorce, there had been no love lost between Isabella and her ex-mother-in-law.

"I'm sorry. You must have been very young then. That must have been difficult." Dr. Wong touched her arm, a natural gesture he probably didn't even realize he made but one that felt very compassionate to her.

It should have been the worst year of her life. But the year Cole had left still ranked as number one in that respect.

"I hadn't realized it had been that long. How is your father doing?" Dr. Lockhart looked concerned—or maybe it was guilty—for letting her father drop off his radar. But Isabella understood. How long could a person be angst-ridden over a lost relationship?

"About the same. Thank you for asking." Isabella thought of the despondent look in her father's eyes last Thursday night when she and Adrian had made their routine twice-a-week visit.

She shook off the sadness, as she always did. No sense in worrying about what couldn't be changed. Neither would gloom and doom raise money for the special games.

Knowing how to change the topic smoothly, Isabella said, "I just love that peachy color on you, Madelaine. It makes your skin glow."

Madelaine accepted the compliment as her due. "And you look lovely as well. Very retro. Yves Saint Laurent?"

"Oleg Cassini." Cassini, Chanel and Givenchy had filled the cedar-lined armoires of the Allante plantation home before hurricane winds had torn half the rotting shingles from the roof last spring.

It had been the last straw. Isabella had had to swallow her pride and accept David's generous offer of one half of his Garden District duplex.

She had to admit that having Adrian's back-up carer right next door had made the whole ordeal of condemning the old mansion a blessing in disguise. Though it still made her heart sink to see the blue plastic tarps tacked over the leaking roof. Her childhood home, once one of the grand dames of the Garden District, was in such bad shape it wouldn't bring much at the sheriff's auction at the end of the month.

"Vintage is so charming." Madelaine drew attention to her own décolletage by touching the intricate opal creation around her neck. "If you don't mind me saying, Isabella, I'll bet your mother always wore pearls with that suit. A double strand would be the perfect accessory for your outfit."

Isabella chose to think of the huge donation Madelaine's family could make instead of the society queen's veiled insult about her vintage clothing and lack of jewelry. She refused to mourn for the magnificent strands of pearls she'd had to sell off, little by little, to pay for her father's medical bills and nursing-home care, just like she refused to mourn for her childhood home.

"I can always count on you for giving top-notch fashion advice, can't I, Madelaine?"

Now, while Madelaine's pride of self puffed out her chest, Isabella should ask for the donation.

A tingle trickled down her spine. A trickle that alerted her that Cole was nearby.

Madelaine spotted him, too. "There's Dr. Lassiter talking with a big guy by the bar. Dad, isn't that Benny Luge, quarterback for our favorite team? Benny's brother, Steve, was in our class in high school. Remember, Isabella? I dated Steve for a while."

"Yes, I remember." She also remembered that Steve, Madelaine and their little clique had treated Cole like a second-class citizen.

"Isabella, did you know Benny flew up to New York so Dr. Lassiter could fix his throwing hand last season?"

"No, I don't keep up with sports, except the special games."

"Cole's a good man," Dr. Lockhart said. "Very generous."

"I doubt the rates he charges professional athletes could be called charity. I guess he's making up for all those years of living off free lunches and scholarships," Madelaine said.

Isabella winced at the snarkiness of Madelaine's tone. Her first inclination was to defend Cole, as she always had when they'd been in their teens. Although she had been pathetically shy, mean-spiritedness toward Cole had been the one thing that could make her stand up to a crowd. But Cole didn't need her defense, did he?

So why did Cole still bring out the fire in her when she wanted him to have no effect on her at all?

Dr. Lockhart looked over his glasses at them both. "You probably haven't heard, since Dr. Lassiter keeps his contributions quietly anonymous, but for every celebrity he and his teams treat, they make a point of treating at least two underprivileged patients."

Wong nodded, adding, "He's been consulting with me on a charity case, a young fireman who has a hand injury. In fact, he scrubbed in on surgery this morning. We had been hoping to avoid amputation and prosthetics and Dr. Lassiter steered us in a more positive direction. The man is absolutely brilliant."

That Cole was an admired doctor didn't surprise Isabella at all. She had always known Cole would excel at whatever he put his mind to. If only he'd had as much passion for nurturing a family as he did for nurturing his medical prowess, she would have never known the pain of a broken heart.

"Isabella, one of Dr. Lassiter's team has a young son who is showing signs of autism. I'm hoping you'll talk to him about applied behavior analysis." Dr. Lockhart gave her a hopeful smile as he beckoned Cole over.

Her heart skipped a beat when she saw Cole head in their direction.

Before she could figure out how to move on gracefully, Dr. Lockhart was introducing them. "Cole, do you remember Isabella Allante? She's the therapist I was telling you about. My daughter has reminded me that all of you went to school together."

"Yes, I remember Bella." Cole gave her a reserved, wary nod. "We renewed our acquaintance when we bumped into each other at the games a few days ago."

What did he expect her to do? Publicly force him to acknowledge his son, then demand fourteen years of paternity payments? She had more class than that.

Madelaine widened her eyes at them as if she'd just caught them kissing under the bleachers. "That's right. You two were an item for a while during your last year of high school."

A close-up photo of Adrian flashed on the screen.

"Isn't that your son, Isabella?" Madelaine pointed to the photo. "How old is he now?"

Isabella made a quick study of her son. He looked so much like Cole at fourteen.

Madelaine narrowed her eyes as she started to put the pieces of Isabella's timeline together. With her nose for gossip, she would have the puzzle worked out by the end of the evening.

Only the immediate Beautemps family knew Adrian wasn't one of their own, and only David and his mother knew about Cole. After all these years of letting everyone make the assumption that Adrian was David's son, was her secret about to be revealed? Her mind boggled at the ripple effect that would have.

She worded her answer carefully. "He's in his last year of middle school." No need to mention that he'd been held back a few years to try to match his classmates' maturity levels.

Without glancing his way, she felt Cole study her, evaluate her, take a step closer to her so she could feel his body radiate with heat. Or was that the force of his personality that made her own body hot?

Damn. Why did Cole have to come back? She could have lived the rest of her life in peace without ever seeing him again. She had been totally satisfied with her life until he'd shown up. Okay, maybe not totally satisfied. But she had plenty going on in her life without needing a man in it, especially this man who made her feel a restlessness she hadn't felt in over fifteen years.

"If you'll excuse me, I need a drink." She turned on her heel to head to the open bar and Cole followed. Snagging two glasses of sparkling white wine, he handed her one.

She almost refused, but that would mean she cared.

She didn't want to care. Didn't want to react to the overpowering maleness of him. Didn't want to think of the string of lonely nights behind her or the infinite ones that stretched before her.

No other man had ever made her feel this yearning, this need to be filled.

As she coached her patients, she would perform the outward motions with the intention of changing inner emotions.

As if Cole were a random stranger, Isabella accepted the crystal flute from him. When his warm fingers brushed hers, she almost dropped her glass. Just a remembered physiological reaction, she scolded herself. Nothing significant there. Certainly nothing to be acted on either positively or negatively. Still, she took a step away.

"Bella, someone called my cellphone this afternoon. No message. Just a hang-up. Since I gave Adrian my cellphone number, I thought it might be him." He rattled off the number.

"That's our home phone. He's never done that before. He doesn't generally reach out to make contact like that." Absently, Isabella took a deep drink of her champagne, not caring that she should sip instead of gulp. If it had truly been Adrian, the phone call was a huge breakthrough.

Overcome with too many opposing emotions, she fought to find words to fill the silence. Any inane utterance would do.

But she was as mute as her son.

"Are you all right?" Cole's voice was deeper now than it had been. And clipped around the edges, as if he was too busy to allow his natural Southern drawl to play out.

"Fine. Just fine." What do you care if I'm not? she wanted to challenge him.

She wanted to break the connection between them even more. No muss, no fuss. Simply walk away from a situation that could get complicated fast.

Was that what Cole had been thinking when he'd deserted her while she'd slept all those years ago?

She couldn't make herself leave him.

"I don't know why Adrian would call you." Except, in his imagination, you're his hero.

"There's no emergency?"

Did he sound disgruntled? Too busy to take a phone call from his own son?

"No. Nothing like that. I'll tell him not to bother you again." Which would be a major setback for Adrian. "You shouldn't have given him your number if you didn't want him to use it."

"I didn't mean that at all. He can call me anytime, although I can't always answer it. If you could explain that to him…"

"You can explain it to him yourself. Although Adrian doesn't like to talk much, his hearing is just fine."

"Then I'll need to work on my one-sided conversations."

Would he really put forth the effort? Or would he realize how frustrating it could be to try to communicate with Adrian, and then drop out of their lives as quickly as he'd dropped in?

Isabella ran her thumb across her hangnail as the decisions of motherhood tore at her. Having a father in his life would mean the world to Adrian. But consistency was key to Adrian's peace of mind. How could she protect her son?

"Don't make promises you don't intend to keep." She found herself standing so close to Cole his body heat warmed her.

Craning her neck to look up into Cole's eyes, she refused to take that first step back, just as he also refused to give ground. Invading each others' personal space felt so provoking, so intimate that every nerve ending cried out to close the gap between them.

"I always keep my promises."

"Then you've changed." She rubbed at her throbbing temple before she pinned him with a stare. "Cole Lassiter, if you disappoint my son, you'll rue the day you ever returned to New Orleans."

He was silent as a muscle worked in his jaw. Finally, he said, "You're a good mother, Bella." He leaned in so close, his breath tickled her ear. "Do you know how your eyes spark when you're passionate? You've become quite a woman, Isabella Allante."

The drawl was back and so were all the conflicting emotions for Cole she'd attempted to forget. His voice caressed her as if he'd reached out and stroked his hand down her spine.

Isabella would have taken a sip of her drink to fill the silence but didn't trust herself to be steady enough to keep from spilling it.

She couldn't stop herself from looking him over, taking in the man he had become. Every inch of him, from his dark shadowed face to his broad shoulders and long-fingered hands oozed testosterone. The very scent of him made her ache for his touch.

What would his hands feel like, cupping her breasts, as they had once done?

She moved, shifting in her heels, because she had to. To stand still with all that need coursing through her would be to come apart.

He gave her a sideways half smile, half smirk as if he knew how he affected her. "Would you like to sit?"

No, I would like to take you to my bed. Her libido was stronger now than it had ever been as a teenager. No question that Cole was the cause. No one else had ever come close to affecting her this way.

"No. I would not like to sit." Having to form a coherent answer kick-started her logic and control. What was she doing, letting her baser emotions run away like that? She didn't have the luxury of letting go. She had responsibilities, duties and a few drops of pride left.

Like she'd done so many times in her life, Isabella concentrated on getting through the moment, leaving the future to untangle itself.

Cole would be gone soon. She would help Adrian grow past his disappointment that his fictional image of Daddy didn't live up to reality. And they would get on with their lives with nothing but another memory of Cole to bury in her boneyard of hopes gone awry.

CHAPTER FOUR

COLE watched myriad emotions cross Bella's eyes—worry, determination, anger, passion...then stone-cold nothing. Apparently she could turn her emotions on and off much more easily than he could. Although those vestiges of passion intrigued him.

More than intrigued him. Enticed him.

But that passion had been replaced with total dispassion in the blink of an eye. History repeating itself.

He should walk away, resigned that Bella would forever be a part of his past that could not be resolved.

Instead, he found himself gazing into her eyes, past the world-weariness, past the guardedness, past the crystal shards sharp enough to cut into a man's soul, searching into the past for a sign of the love they had promised to hold sacred—until she'd married another man.

Searching for something, anything, to keep her by his side, he said, "I enjoyed your speech last Thursday." He took a sip of champagne even though he detested the sparkling taste. "You're not as shy as you used to be."

She had been shy in public, but in private, in his little one-room efficiency apartment on the wrong side of town, she had been anything but shy in bed. Not only had she been generous in her lovemaking, she'd been open with her words of love as well.

Seeing Isabella now was stirring up all kinds of forgotten memories.

"I'm not a lot of things I used to be." She toasted him and took a deep sip, obviously enjoying the bubbles sliding down her throat. "You missed the whole message and only heard the closing remarks."

"You noticed when I came and went?"

Telling her absentminded father the age-old ploy that she was spending the weekend with female friends, she had stayed with him instead. That whole senior year they had talked of their future together. The weekend before he'd left for NYU for pre-med she had promised to be his wife as soon as he could support a family. As she'd lain asleep, worn out from a night of lovemaking, he had kissed her on the cheek and promised to do everything he could so they could be together as soon as possible.

"You weren't very subtle about it."

"Even after all these years, subtlety isn't one of my specialties."

Less than two weeks later he'd received her engagement announcement. She hadn't even had the decency to send it herself, but had had her future mother-in-law drop the newspaper clipping into the mail for her.

"You never saw the need for nuance, did you, Cole? I'll bet you fit in real well in New York."

"Plain-speaking leaves less room for misunderstandings."

David's mother, the matriarch of the Beautemps family, had added her own sentiment, written in her precise handwriting on monogrammed heavyweight stationery: "I understand the upcoming nuptials may come as a surprise to you, but this wedding has been planned for quite a while. I am sure you wish for a secure and stable life for Isabella. Please respect that she has found that and more in David. Our family can give her what you cannot. Please accept the

*enclosed check as a token of the Beautemps' wishes for a se-
cure and stable future for you as well."*

No subtlety wasted there.

She took a deep drink from her glass. "I was surprised to
see you in my lecture."

"I was actually trying to attend the lecture before yours,
but got the times wrong."

At her frown, he realized that hadn't sounded very flattering. He hadn't meant to be rude.

She used to bring out the best in him. Did she bring out
the worst now?

He flagged down a passing waiter to put his glass on the
empty tray. "I grabbed a copy of your notes for my office
manager. Her daughter may have development issues."

"So you don't plan to read them yourself?"

"I saw your credentials listed in your bio. Impressive."

*The check had been the first of many communications he
had torn to shreds. He'd taken out his anger, his hurt and his
humiliation on anything postmarked with the New Orleans
mail stamp.*

"Tell your office manager there's a website URL to eval-
uation services for each area of the country on the last page
of the notes."

"Where is your office?"

"You need my services?"

"I might want to make a referral or two."

*First he'd ripped her letters to pieces and scattered them
to the winds, watching the waters of the Hudson River carry
them away. As he'd stood on the bank, watching, he'd felt as
if pieces of his heart were sinking below the murky surface
with each melting piece of paper.*

He thought she wasn't going to tell him until she reached
into her purse and gave him a card. "In the Garden District."

"In your childhood neighborhood, then."

"Yes, in a historic home converted into small offices."

"I went by your old house."

"It's for sale. You saw the sign?"

"I know that must hurt."

Then, as the weather had turned cold, he would burn them in his tiny balcony grill and warm his hands over the ashes.

Bella shrugged away his concern. "Sometimes things just don't work out as you expect them to."

He had erased all her phone messages without listening to them. He didn't know if he could have survived her sweet voice trying to justify, trying to explain how a boy with his background could never measure up to the Beautemps.

"The experts would tell us to cherish the good memories and let go of the bad." He had thought he'd had his past under control—until he'd set foot on Louisiana soil. Now he kept meeting it on every street corner.

When he'd finally torn up that last letter, unread, he'd written a letter of his own, telling her in the kindest way he could to get on with life. She'd stopped trying to contact him. And he had mourned.

Was that a flicker of remembrance for the passion that had once bound them together?

"Why, Cole?" Bella asked all his unspoken questions.

Before he could sort out answers he didn't have, Dr. Wong came up to them. "Dance with me, Isabella?"

"This dance is already taken." Using the same fierceness Cole had used to back down the street gangs of his youth, he glared at the man who would likely be his business partner in the near future.

Rebelliousness set Bella's jaw, but Wong had already bowed out and turned away before she could protest. "Maybe I wanted to dance with Dr. Wong."

Most women would protest against Cole's high-handedness

and rightfully so. But tonight the caveman inside him wouldn't allow Dr. Wong to put his hands on Bella.

He blamed his Neanderthal behavior on still trying to find his balance. Seeing her that afternoon had been such a shock. She had a career. She had a son. She had a life.

"Dance with me instead." Without waiting for her acquiescence, he put his hand on her back to lead her onto the dance floor. Cole counted on her reluctance to make a scene to keep her from protesting.

He read her right. She glanced around, saw no easy way out, and chose to avoid a scene. Why else would she dance with him? No, she hadn't changed that much. The old Bella had always done what society had expected of her. Like marrying David Beautemps.

A wave of jealously flooded through him for the gift the Beautemps had been given. David had had a wonderful, intelligent and beautiful woman and a son any man would be proud to call his own. They had seemed to be the perfect couple. What had gone wrong with their marriage? And why should it matter to him?

He just knew he had to touch her or he would never be healed of the deep wound she'd left in his heart.

As he wrapped his arms around her, Cole felt as if fragments of himself fitted into place. There was a fullness, a wholeness about Bella pressed against his body. Automatically, their bodies fell into rhythm to the strains of a slow Louis Armstrong number.

He knew why he was dancing with her. Illogical though it was, he couldn't stand the sight of another man holding her—and he didn't feel like dredging up the strength of will to push away his baser tendencies. Not tonight, not after all the turmoil his homecoming had stirred in him, when all he'd wanted to do was bring comfort and cures to those who needed it the most. After all the pain he'd had to work through, he was due a bit of self-indulgence, wasn't he?

But why did she clutch him equally strongly?

Was it so wrong of her to pretend, just for a few minutes, that life had turned out differently? She was so exhausted, emotionally and mentally as well as physically. Would it hurt to steal a moment's respite?

Bella clung to Cole, following his lead like she'd done all those years ago.

In her high heels, she was the perfect height to nestle her head on his shoulder. Her feet automatically fell into step as he guided them around the dance floor.

She closed her eyes, letting Cole's masculine closeness seep into her. His arms provided a sanctuary in the crowd.

For just a few minutes she would allow herself to have no responsibilities, no decisions to make, nothing but Cole in her world—the world she had always fantasized about. She didn't even have to worry about where to take her next step, with Cole leading the way.

With a little imagination she could almost hear his heart beat beneath her ear.

His touch was so familiar yet so foreign. His hands cupped hers the way they had in the past, but his palms felt bigger, more encompassing, and his fingers felt more sensitive against hers.

The tingle was the same, but more so. Not only did electricity race along the surface of her body but a bigger energy that was uniquely Cole dove beneath the surface to enmesh with her own flagging energy.

Her soul fed from his.

Soul mates—in another lifetime, perhaps. Now two old acquaintances with the spectre of an unacknowledged son between them.

She found the strength to lift her head, breaking the connection.

"You fit me exactly like you used to." Cole maneuvered them around a less graceful couple. "You always felt so fragile, so delicate. After all these years you're still a wisp of a woman."

"I assume you're trying to flatter me but you're taking the wrong tack. You don't know me anymore, Cole."

She pushed herself away enough to look him in the eye. Thinking of the way he had superciliously led her onto the dance floor, she decided to test her own influence over him.

"I'm not who I used to be." Deliberately, she licked her lips and watched his pupils darken with desire. "I'm better."

Knowing that she could still rouse Cole's desire, even after all these years, did much to soothe her bruised ego. But she really didn't have time for his games.

As if she drew the strength from him to push him away, Bella put her hands between them. "I've got work to do."

Not breaking rhythm, Cole whispered in her ear, "What work? This is a party."

"It's a fundraiser. I've got funds to raise."

"How much do you need?"

"You can't just write a check."

"Oh, but I can. Tell me how much this dance will cost me."

Not as much as getting away from me cost some faceless scholarship committee, she wanted to retort. But she didn't make scenes in public.

The Allantes may have taken a big tumble down the high-society ladder, but that didn't mean she'd lost her dignity as well as her social position.

"Giving to the games is about an emotional commitment as well as a monetary one." She looked up at the hard planes of his face and gave him a twisted smile. "And you can't give what you don't have."

Turning away after delivering her coup de grâce, Isabella was brought up short by a waiter with a note in his white-gloved hand. "Excuse the interruption, Ms. Allante, but the caller said it was urgent."

Isabella read the note: "Adrian cut his hand. Meet me at Tulane's Emergency Room."

Cole took the note from her and glanced over it. "I'll drive you."

Arguing would only waste time.

Isabella sat tensely, her hands clasped in her lap, as Cole maneuvered through traffic. Cole could have tried to ease Bella's worries with platitudes but she had reached over and switched off his radio the minute he'd cranked up his rented BMW, a strong indication she didn't want distractions. He took the hint.

Now she sat, shoulders tense, her hands clasped in her lap, her focus on the scenery outside the passenger window, clearly not receptive to communication. She'd been like that the day she'd waited to learn her mother's fate.

In the hospital's reflection garden, she'd sat on the edge of the wooden bench, clasping and unclasping her hands until he'd laced his fingers through hers. Then she'd held on tight, tighter than he could have imagined such a small girl could grip, staring out into the azalea-filled garden. And he'd sat with her in case she needed him. Three hours in the hot, humid mosquito-laden afternoon, until a chaplain had brought the message that Bella's mother was dead.

Without speaking, she'd moved over, closing the gap that separated them until their shoulders had touched as tears had tracked down her face.

When he'd dared to wrap his arm around her, she had leaned into him, giving in to one full sob, then apologized if she'd made him uncomfortable. Politely and mechanically, she had thanked him for waiting before excusing herself to find her father so she could ask what she needed to do next.

That was how everything had been handled in the Allante household, gracious and controlled.

That was why he had never fit in, not with his hot temper and propensity to say what was on his mind. But he'd learned. It had been a lesson hard-won, but he had learned to be just as cool and unemotional as Bella.

And he had to admit that shutting out his emotions kept him from hurting so much in public. How he felt in his private darkness was another matter entirely.

Cole barely had his car parked and out of gear before Isabella was climbing out. Even in her high heels she took quick strides at just under a run toward the emergency entrance.

At the reception desk she visibly restrained herself, taking a deep breath and swallowing before asking in her cultured tones, "I'm here for my son, Adrian Allante."

Allante? Not Beautemps? But Cole didn't spend time dwelling on Adrian's surname as he followed Bella to the examination room where Adrian was.

Before going in, Bella took another deep breath, then, as if just remembering Cole was there, warned him, "Adrian doesn't respond well to excess emotion."

But her unfocused eyes made Cole momentarily wonder if she were telling him or reminding herself.

Adrian sat on an examination table, rocking back and forth. He fingered his scarf with a bloody hand and held tight to a doctor doll in the other.

The lights were dim and the room quiet. If David Beautemps hadn't moved in the corner chair, Cole would have overlooked him.

David gave her a wan smile and said in a whisper Cole barely heard, "Bella, I'm so sorry. Adrian dropped a picture frame. The glass shattered in large pieces. He cut himself trying to put it back together. I found all the shards, so I don't think there's any in the cut."

"Accidents happen. I'm glad he was with you." She slashed Cole a sharp glance as she said, "David, you always do the right thing."

"The cut isn't that deep but it's rather long. The staff need parental permission before they can stitch it up."

Why couldn't David give parental permission? Because he wasn't Adrian's father?

Was that what had happened to their marriage? Cole couldn't reconcile the Isabella Allante he'd known with a woman who would step outside marriage and have an affair.

But, then, he hadn't known Bella as well as he'd thought he had.

The boy looked nothing like David—or Bella either—yet something about him looked very familiar. Maybe the way he carried himself, or was it in his eyes?

No, Bella wasn't the kind of woman to have one man's child while married to another man. And it was obvious to anyone that David still cared greatly—for both mother and son.

A nurse burst into the room and flipped on the lights.

"How are you today, young man?" she asked in a cheerful bedside voice. "And why are we sitting here in the dark?"

Adrian sped up his rocking as he started to thump the doctor doll on the table. His face clouded while his eyes blanked, like his inner conscious was separating from his body.

Behind him, Bella flipped off the light and walked over to stand in front of Adrian, looking past him instead of into his eyes and taking long, slow breaths.

Quietly, David clued the young nurse in. "Adrian has autism and feels better when the room isn't so bright. We understand you'll need light to work in. Is it possible to examine him with just a strong light beam on his hand?"

Cole got the strong impression Bella and David had worked as a team many times. Jealousy stabbed him, even though the emotion defied logic. Bella hadn't been his to have and to hold for a decade and a half now. Rationally, he was glad, for both Bella's and Adrian's sakes that they had David to rely on.

The nurse blinked, then rallied. "Sure. We'll give it a try. But I'm afraid it will be a while. We've just had a major trauma, a bus accident, and everyone needs to be triaged so we won't have a doctor available for a bit."

Meanwhile, Adrian began echoing his mother's breaths even as he slowed the beat of the doctor doll against the table. Cole was all too aware of the surreptitious attention Adrian gave him and made sure his own attitude reflected nothing but calm.

"I've recently been granted hospital privileges here. I can take care of Adrian's cut."

The young nurse took a moment to peer at Cole in the dimness of the room. "Yes, Dr. Lassiter, I recognize you. I'm sure you don't recognize me as I was behind a mask at the time, but I assisted in your case."

"I'm surprised you recognize me, for the same reason."

"Everyone knows you, Doctor. The work you did for that fireman was phenomenal."

Cole shifted his shoulders. He'd never been comfortable with compliments. Deep down, he would always be the dirt-poor shrimper's son, raised to know his place.

"Dr. Lassiter, I'm not needed for the triage. I can assist if you need me to."

"Thank you, Nurse. I can use your help."

She moved in close and spoke so only he could hear. "Anything you need, Doctor."

Cole heard the unspoken message in her tone of voice. He wasn't new to being propositioned. But he was new to not even being the slightest bit intrigued.

Instead, he focused on his patient.

"Adrian, I need to look at your cut and assess how deep it is. I know all these procedures may be uncomfortable for you but I know you can bear it, too."

Adrian looked to the right and down in acknowledgment.

The little niggle in the back of Cole's mind took on a full-blown hammer strike as he now recognized the obvious.

Now Cole knew where he'd seen the boy's eyes before—in his own mirror. Certainty filled him. When Isabella had married David, she had been pregnant with his child.

Adrian was his son.

Why had Bella kept the truth from him? He had missed so much.

His hot temper flared. He'd thought he'd left that depth of passion behind along with his broken heart all those years ago. But he had his son to think of first.

Cole deliberately tamped down his reactions while inwardly he ran through the questions he would pin Isabella with the moment he could get her alone.

With great self-discipline he mentally forced minute details of the case at hand into the spotlight and made everything else in the room fade away.

"Adrian, I need light to see your hand better. I'm going to turn on this lamp. Close your eyes if it helps."

Obediently, Adrian squeezed his eyes tight while Cole flipped on the bright examination lamp.

"Now, I need you to open your hand and lay it on this tray." He covered a metal tray with sterile paper and positioned it between Adrian and himself.

When Adrian didn't move, Cole sent a quick glance toward

Bella while avoiding looking directly at her. He needed to keep her out of his thoughts to keep his composure.

They would talk after he cared for Adrian.

"Adrian, your mother is going to guide your hand to the tray and open your fingers so I can see your injury." He gave Bella a firm nod.

Isabella saw the cut was just as David had described, shallow but long.

Putting the scarf between her and Adrian, she cupped his hand and peeled back his fingers. Tense situations made Adrian more sensitive to skin-to-skin touch than he usually was.

"Antiseptic and a bead of skin glue will be sufficient," he directed to the nurse who got him the requested supplies.

With Cole administering to him, Adrian didn't even flinch.

For her son's sake, Bella was glad Cole was there.

When Cole moved in close and bent to apply the glue, his hand brushed hers. His touch was like electricity, raising tingles along her arm that shivered all the way through her. She had to fight herself to keep her stoicism.

Cole didn't even seem to notice her, much less her reaction as he focused on Adrian.

"I'm going to wrap your hand to keep you from moving it too much, so the edges of the cut can seal better," he said to Adrian. "Don't get it wet. You can take the wrap off tomorrow morning."

To tamp down her emotional side, Isabella focused on her rational side, appreciating the way Cole spoke directly to her son. Because Adrian didn't respond verbally, many people didn't talk to him. Instead, they spoke to her as if she needed to relay the message. It was a natural instinct but not an accurate one.

Procedure complete, Cole stretched his neck from side to side and grimaced. The behavior therapist in Isabella wanted to offer ergonomic observations but she kept her medical opinions to herself. Knowing when and how to dispense advice and how to keep her personal distance was a big part of her therapy training and an area she usually excelled in.

But Cole, standing this close to her, made keeping her emotional distance difficult.

"Thank you, Nurse. We're done here." Cole dismissed the nurse who obviously wanted to take their relationship beyond the hospital walls. Isabella applauded his professionalism while she ignored the possessiveness that kept trying to surface.

"Let's all three of us step into the hallway," Cole said it more as an order than a suggestion.

While she would usually take umbrage at his brusqueness, this time she understood. That was how doctors were: authoritative and totally sure of themselves. They needed to be confident to make the split-second decisions they had to make. But the sharpness of his tone alarmed her.

She led the way, with a nervous glance back at her son. "Is there a problem with Adrian? I thought he only had a small cut."

"Adrian will be fine. This isn't about his hand." Then Cole overstepped his physician's role, "David, if you would take Adrian home now, I'll drive Bella back to the hotel."

"Who are you to make arrangements for my son or for me?" Isabella challenged, setting free all her pent-up anxiety in the form of righteous anger.

"Our son." Cole pinned her with a glare. His eyes, only moments ago so impassively focused on his patient, now glowed with the darkness of hell. "Bella, we need to talk."

CHAPTER FIVE

ISABELLA felt her world shift under her. Ambulance sirens sounded like they came from within her instead of from the entrance to the emergency room.

Cole looked shocked. His whole attitude shouted that he hadn't known. How could that be?

"Why now? Where were you fifteen years ago?" she forced through her tight throat. Her words sounded rasping and raw even to her own ears.

All rational thought fled, including her own earlier decision to confront Cole and demand he either acknowledge Adrian or go away.

Every nerve fiber screamed to protect herself, protect her heart, protect her carefully constructed and controlled world. "Later. It's been a long night—a long week. We'll talk later." Later, with the safety of a phone line between them, it wouldn't hurt so much, would it?

She looked to David for support.

"This conversation is long overdue, Isabella," David said.

David's pronouncement felt like the ultimate betrayal.

Cole crossed his arms, looking imposing. "We can do this in private or we can do it right here."

How could she expose those old wounds to the man who had created them? No, she would not let him call the shots.

She crossed her arms as well, but in self-protection rather

than in an attempt to intimidate. "Or we can not do it at all. After all these years, there's no need to discuss anything."

As her voice quavered, she acknowledged self-preservation quickly overtaking rationality.

"Isabella..." David took a glance back at Adrian sitting in the dark, fondling his scarf "...you need to get the air cleared. For Adrian's sake as well as your own."

David had never deserted her before. But now he was taking Cole's side. Still, they were sobering words. David was half right—*for Adrian's sake.*

Every boy needed a father, and her boy needed one more than most.

She would do anything for her son—even cut out her own heart and hand it over on a silver platter. "Fine. We'll talk now." Emotionally overwhelmed, she walked in a daze to the parking lot.

Inside Cole's car, Bella felt claustrophobic. Very precisely, Cole drove to the hotel, his neck and shoulders stiff, his knuckles white on the steering wheel. Even the heavy air felt permeated with Cole's anger.

How could he not have known? She'd left messages on his cellphone, sent letters through the mail, pleaded with his friends to have him call her, right up to the night before the wedding.

But her blistering anger had burnt out many years ago, leaving behind only ashes. At least that was what she'd told herself. Apparently, she had only banked the embers. Now she could feel a slow burn flicker to life deep in her core.

As soon as he'd parked, he stalked around the car and opened the door for her. He didn't put out his hand to assist her but she wouldn't have taken it if he had. This was not a one-sided story.

While he didn't touch her, Cole stayed close enough that she could feel the fury coming off his skin in waves. At the bank of elevators, he punched in his floor number without discussion, and escorted Bella to his suite.

At his door, she thought about turning around and leaving, but she wasn't that girl who couldn't stand up for herself anymore. If confrontation was what Cole wanted, confrontation was what he would get.

Once inside his rooms, Cole raked his hand through his hair. Rage throbbed at his temples. The effort he exerted to control his temper made his throat ache with the strain.

Bella stood with her back to the door, her hands strangling her purse strap as if she wished it was his neck in her fists. She held her chin high, daring him to challenge her. Her stance was strong, her legs long on her petite frame.

Her legs. What a distraction.

How could he hate her and want her at the same time?

No, he didn't hate her, even though he'd tried all those years ago. What did he feel for her? Right now, he would go with desire and leave it at that.

But he'd left her before and it had been the wrong thing to do.

"I don't know where to start." He paced the length of his suite, putting distance between them. Then, as if he couldn't help himself, he paced back, closing the space between them.

When Isabella flinched, he took a tighter hold on himself and backed off a half dozen steps, giving her plenty of breathing room.

Her jaw jutted and her lips pressed together, such a sharp contrast to the softness of her upswept hair beginning to fall in wisps down her neck. Why didn't she say something? Anything? What would it take to ease the tightness of her lips?

The distracting urge to cover her mouth with his own could easily turn into an obsession.

"I would never hurt you, no matter how angry I become. Don't you know that about me?" he asked in a restrained, hoarse whisper.

Still she looked wary. "What does either of us know about the other anymore?"

I know you make me burn hotter than I've ever burnt before. That she was the mother of his child made him want her even more. "Did you know you were carrying my baby when you married him?"

"You know I did, Cole. That was the reason I married David. It was in the letters." The hard stare she gave him seared him to the bone. "You didn't read them, did you?"

Cole thought back to all the letters he had torn to shreds without opening. And to that final terse letter he'd sent her. Even after all these years, he remembered every word he'd written: "Everything between us is in the past. You've made your choice. Now live with it and leave me alone to make my own life." He'd enclosed a copy of the engagement announcement in the letter to emphasize his point, then dropped it into the mailbox, swearing never to look back.

Fury flooded him—a self-consuming inferno in his veins—as understanding flooded through him. Not knowing about his son was all his own fault.

He ached as if all the anger in his heart had turned into razor-sharp shards of glass and was now being carried with his blood supply.

He had done this to himself—and to Bella and his son.

The pain was excruciating. He hurt so bad, he couldn't hold himself up anymore. Leaning his back against the wall, he admitted, "I tore them up without reading them."

Bella asked again that all-encompassing question she had asked earlier before they'd danced. "Why, Cole?"

"I had no idea you could possibly be pregnant. We were careful." As soon as he'd said it, he knew they hadn't been.

In their youth they hadn't understood that coitus interruptus had a very high failure rate as birth control, especially for teenage boys.

"Not always." Bella gave him a lopsided smile, remembering, too, no doubt. "You didn't read even one? Weren't you even curious about what I had to say?"

"I was too—" Nothing but truth here. After all these years, they both deserved nothing but the unvarnished truth. "I was too wounded. I was struggling, trying to find my way in a strange place when I'd never even been outside New Orleans before. When I wasn't studying, I was waiting tables. I didn't have the time or energy to grieve for our relationship and I thought that's all those letters would be. Just a rehash of why you didn't love me anymore."

He reflected on all the phone messages he'd erased without listening to them first, the friends from home he'd berated when they'd even tried to bring up Bella's name. He'd even broken ties with his best friend when that friend had insisted Cole really needed to call Bella.

"Did David know before you married?" Cole twisted his neck back and forth and shrugged his shoulders, trying to stop the terrible ache that throbbed from the base of his skull, radiated down his arm and made his fingertips buzz. "Did he know you were carrying my child?"

"Of course he did. What kind of person do you think I am? Did you think I would try to fool him?" Bella's normally stoic face flushed with uncharacteristic passion.

The quiet, reserved Bella he used to know had so rarely shown high emotion, except in bed. As reticent as she was in public, she was bold and magnificent in private—or at least she had been at eighteen. Did she still get a rosy glow all over when she was satisfied, or was she too jaded now? And why was Cole thinking of those bygone days?

"So David married you to cover for my mistake." A roaring vortex of possessiveness rushed through him at the thought of any man claiming his son—or his woman. He turned to stare out the window to avoid glaring at her. He could see Bella's reflection in the dark glass, her face stark in shadows and light.

"My son is not a mistake."

"Of course he's not. The mistake was my sloppy form of birth control. I take full responsibility."

"It's a bit late for that." Anger edged Bella's controlled voice.

He didn't need to see her reflection in the glass to know she moved toward him. He could feel it in the tingling down his spine.

"You turn your back on me, Cole? You shut me out now? You're the one who wanted this conversation."

He whipped around to face her, knowing he couldn't hide the emotions on his face—and not wanting to anymore. She should see his anger for wanting and not having, his anguish over leaving her, his soul-grieving destitution for all he'd missed. "What I want is my son."

Bella. Magnificent in her fury. So full of emotion it glittered in her amethyst eyes, daring him to answer her challenge. Could there be any stronger aphrodisiac?

Bella braced her hands on her hips. "He is my son. All you've done is contribute the sperm."

The stark reality of Bella's statement hit Cole like a glove to the face.

Since he'd seen that engagement announcement, Cole had never desired a family, never wanted the ties, the responsibility, the permanence. Now, he craved that bond so strongly he felt he'd never be whole and healed again without it. Heaven help him, that craving wasn't only for healing. It was for Bella, in every form a man could crave a woman.

He swallowed, trying to get a handle on his passions. "So

you made a few attempts then let it drop? Why, Bella? Why didn't you at least contact me after the divorce?"

"If you really want to discuss this, Cole, why don't we sit, like civilized people?"

"Civilized. It's been a while since anyone called my civility into question. But, then, it's been a while since I've felt this feral." He turned and stood next to a chair while gesturing toward the couch. "Won't you please take a seat? Is that civil enough for an Allante?"

Bella took steps toward the couch, but continued to stand as if she was ready to bolt at any second, just like she'd done when she'd been a skittish teenager. That kind of vulnerability had called forth the protector in him while it called the bully in others.

She looked him straight in the eye. "You always did take offense where none was meant. I'd have thought you would have gotten past that by now."

He laughed at himself, a short, tight burst. "Me, too. You bring out the old reactions in me."

But that wasn't true. Those had been the reactions of a boy. Now his reactions were man-size.

He ached for her like he had never ached for another woman, even after all these years. This was no teenage lust. This was a full-grown yearning, much deeper, much more intense. Bella was the woman who evoked his deepest desires.

Now he understood why he had never been able to find that elusive satisfaction to his yearning. He'd been looking in all the wrong places.

Isabella sat on the edge of her seat, too uptight to bend her spine even the slightest degree. With all the adrenaline rushing through her, she had to force herself to stay seated, though she wanted to pace. But her steps had carried her closer and closer to Cole even while her mind told her body to walk away.

Cole, folded into a chair too small for his large frame, watched every move she made. The intensity in his dark brown eyes turned them to polished obsidian.

The caregiver in her wanted to relieve the pain etched into his face, smooth the furrows of his brow. The female in her wanted to run her hand along the sharp plane of his cheek, feel the roughness of the shadow of beard that emphasized his maleness.

Instead, she clenched her fingers even tighter, feeling the leather of her purse straps bite into her hand.

Why, after all this time, did she still feel the pull between them? It had always been this way, since the first time she'd spotted him wearing scuffed, secondhand shoes, his hair too long and his eyes hinting of a world she had never seen before—the ultimate bad boy. He'd been sitting alone in the school cafeteria, eating the mediocre food as if he hadn't eaten in days, daring anyone and everyone to come close to him—except her.

She had felt she had no choice but to go to him. Exactly like she felt now—but now she knew how dangerous he could be for her.

Taking over every inch of chair space, he looked just as out of place now—and just as hungry. The way he looked at her, she felt like a kitten thrown into a starving lion's den.

She had thought with each of them taking a seat, she wouldn't feel so overpowered by his size. But it wasn't his physical size—it was the massiveness of his presence that made her feel so diminutive.

Cole emanated an essence so electric that she felt like a radical electron being pushed and pulled around his orbit.

What did she feel for Cole Lassiter? Anger wasn't the right emotion.

She looked at him, really looked at him, trying to find that boy she'd known beneath the man's exterior, the wild boy who would be tamed only by her. The soulful boy who would listen for hours when everyone else thought she had nothing to say. The knightly boy who'd treated her like a precious princess when everyone else found her mousy and dull.

It definitely wasn't in the cast of his jaw or the clench of his mouth, once so determined but now so grim.

She searched his eyes for a flicker of who he used to be—of who they used to be.

He blinked, letting loose the full extent of his emotions, making her shiver.

Fifteen years ago, Cole's passion could carry her beyond her everyday world to a place of ecstasy. His eyes still flashed with that same promise, that same passion, that same desire that used to make her feel so alive.

As he stared at her right now, she felt the same way.

She had too many emotions roiling around to sort them out right now. And soon Cole would be gone, so why should she expend the energy? She would answer his questions, he would leave, and that would be the end of this unexpected encounter.

"You wanted to talk?" she challenged him. "Talk."

A muscle worked in his jaw as he leaned forward, rested his elbows on his knees and tapped his fingertips together.

The way he held his neck and shoulders, the angle was off. She'd seen that posture before. It meant pain, physical pain. No doubt this emotionally painful conversation intensified it.

More gently, she said, "No secrets between us. I'll tell you whatever you want to know."

He stopped tapping. "What about the engagement? One Saturday night I kissed you goodbye, expecting to have a long-distance relationship. Two weeks later I got a letter with your engagement notice in it. You never even gave me a chance."

She gave him an ironic smile. "I had my first bout of morning sickness the morning you left. My mind-body studies would say that was my way of reacting to losing you."

"Turn off the therapist, Bella. You're using it as a barrier between us."

She flushed, one part anger at being castigated by Cole, two parts shame at Cole being right.

"Who do you think you are, Cole Lassiter, to tell me what to do?" What should have sounded like rebellious independence sounded petulant instead.

"I'm the father of your child. You owe me answers." His eyes reflected his need to know, his passion for the truth.

Hadn't they wounded each other enough with their failure to communicate on so many levels? Wasn't it time to acknowledge and take responsibility for the scars they had left on each other's lives?

She licked her lips, wishing she had a glass of water to hide behind.

Cole's eyes focused on her mouth, so intense she had to put her fingers to her lips to break his stare. Under her fingertips, her lips buzzed with sensitivity. He could command a response without even touching her.

She swallowed her own response, so thick in her throat, and told him the truth as best she could. "I didn't realize I was pregnant until later that week. I thought I had food poisoning or something." She'd been so naive back then. "My father is the one who figured it out. He called David's mother and that's when the problems began."

She had been so confused and so embarrassed. Her gentle, loving, overwhelmed father who had tried to nurture and guide his motherless girl-child the best he could had been just as baffled about what to do next as she had been.

"Why didn't you call me?"

"I had no way to contact you those first few days. You were traveling and you didn't have a phone." She had been so confused, so scared.

Cole's fisted fingers clenched tight. "David's mother found me. The engagement announcement was waiting for me when I checked into my dorm."

"I don't know how she knew where to send the letter, or even why she would think she should send it to you. I was so careful to—"

"To hide your socially unacceptable boyfriend."

"I wasn't supposed to be seeing you. Every time I snuck out to stay with you, I told my father I was staying with girl-friends."

Isabella felt her face flush as Cole's accusation hit home. Seeing Cole on the sly had felt wild and rebellious when she had always been so meek and biddable. Stolen moments with Cole had been the most exhilarating time of her young life. In fact, being around him now still made her feel that way.

"Yeah, I know." He shifted then looked her in the eye. "I guess something good came out of all that social class prej-udice. I used all your friends' snide remarks and insults to spur me on so I could prove I was as good as anyone else. Could that be why you agreed to the engagement, Bella? I wasn't good enough?"

"No! Of all the things I was unsure of, that was never one of them." But deep down Bella questioned herself. While she'd never consciously thought about Cole's inability to care for her and baby, had her subconscious reasoned it out?

"Then why the quickie engagement and wedding to David?"

She had a solid answer for that one. "My father and David's mother were trying to protect me."

"What did David's mother have to do with anything?"

"Don't you remember, Cole? Mama and Mrs. Beautemps were best friends. After Mama died, Mrs. Beautemps tried to stand in for her. She took me shopping for my debutante dress, arranged for deportment classes, even included my father and me in all their family vacations and holiday plans."

Cole shook his head and winced. "I was never privy to that part of your life. All we ever had were stolen moments after school."

"Those stolen moments were the highlights of my life. They outweighed all the trips and parties tenfold." She swallowed and admitted, "I was so entranced with you. You were so fascinating, so different from anyone I'd ever known."

"Different. Too different? Is that why you did it, Isabella? You couldn't see yourself forever tied to the bad boy of St. Michael's Prep School?"

"No, Cole." Isabella stopped herself. "At least, not consciously. Truthfully, a life with you was so far beyond my imagination I couldn't wrap my mind around it. That whole time was such a roller-coaster ride."

Even after all these years, Isabella's stomach roiled at the memory of all the tears she had shed into her pillow. "But Mrs. Beautemps assumed the baby was David's and immediately started making wedding plans. She said the sooner, the better to keep the talk to a minimum. Nothing reprehensible there—even the letter David's mother sent to you must have been her way of trying to protect me."

"Stop right there, Bella." Cole held up an imposing hand like a traffic cop. "If she thought the child was David's, why bother to warn me off?"

The suspicion Bella had always tried to ignore could no longer be sidestepped. Still, an old sense of loyalty had her protesting. And then there was the part of the story that belonged to David and she had no right to reveal that. "Mrs. Beautemps loved me like a daughter."

"Loved? As in past tense, used to love?"

"Yes. During the divorce, when I told her that Adrian wasn't David's son, she dropped me from her life. David wanted to claim Adrian, but telling the Beautemps family was the right thing to do. The family inheritance shouldn't go to Adrian. It's meant to stay in the family. That's the reason I didn't list David's name on the birth certificate even though he wanted me to." Isabella still had a bruised place in her heart from the loss of her relationship with her mother-in-law. "I know the revelation caught her off guard, but how could she stop loving me, and stop loving the boy she thought was her grandchild?"

"The same way you stopped loving me." Cole said it as if it were a stone-cold fact.

That was the problem. No matter how hard she had tried to stop feeling anything for him, Cole would always be Bella's first love. And so far she had found no one to take his place. Seeing him now, she was fairly certain no one could take his place.

But he would be gone soon, so what she felt didn't matter, did it?

"So you just blithely went along with the whole plan to marry another man to give my son a father."

"Not at first." Isabella still felt proud of herself for her initial resistance. It had been so unlike her at the time and had been the beginning of her independence. "Mrs. Beautemps put the engagement announcement in the paper before I had time to think about it. I was furious when the announcement came out and I absolutely refused to marry David."

Cole leaned forward on the edge of his chair, as if struggling to keep himself seated. "But you did."

Looking back, it was hard to believe how sheltered and shy she had been. Or maybe not. She'd seen plenty of people, both men and women, who had either withdrawn or gone out of control when they'd lost a parent. Her mother had been the energizing force of their family, while Isabella had been the type of person to withdraw, just like her father.

She looked at the man across from her, the man who had lost his father, mother and brother before she'd ever known him.

Cole was an extraordinary person. For the first time in all these years she sent kind, forgiving thoughts his way.

Gently, she explained, "After you wouldn't return my calls or answer my letters, I received that one single letter from you. When I read it, I knew there was no us anymore. When I explained everything to David, he insisted that we go ahead with the wedding so he could take care of me until I could figure out my life. I felt I had no choice. I was protecting my baby."

"But why didn't you tell me later?"

"Why? At first, everyone assumed Adrian was David's child and David was content to keep it that way. The thought of an heir to carry on the Beautemps name made his family happy, and he pledged to raise Adrian as his own." And Bella had promised to keep David's secret safe. "After the divorce, all our lives were working just fine and I saw no reason to disrupt it."

"So, from the beginning, David just blithely went along with this whole scheme?"

"David has always been my best friend. We would do anything for each other."

"Include sleep with each other?"

"That's none of your business."

She didn't need to explain to Cole that the relationship she and David had was totally platonic. She wasn't David's type. And the only man she'd ever slept with was sitting across from her, glowering at her like she'd done something wrong.

No, she wouldn't be intimidated or second-guessed. "I did what was best at the time."

As if Cole finally realized the magnitude of all Bella had gone through, he rubbed his hand across his face. "Maybe you did, Bella. Maybe you did." Cole let out a deep breath that seemed to come from the depths of his understanding. "I'm sorry. I should have been there for you." He looked into her eyes. "I will take care of you from now on."

But it was too late, too condescending, too little. He hadn't even bothered to read the letters while she'd cried herself to sleep every night for weeks.

"Just like that?" She snapped her fingers. "Because you say it, it becomes so? Well, let me tell you something, Cole Lassiter, I've learned how to stand up for myself while you were away and I don't need you anymore."

"What about my son, Bella?"

"He doesn't need you either."

"What if I need him?" He rose from his chair. "What if I need you?"

His eyes, his voice, his intensity, everything about him made her quiver as energy sparked through her.

One night. He owed her that much.

She stood and took two steps forward, bringing her within inches of his touch. "Prove it."

CHAPTER SIX

ALL those nights, all those years, of loneliness, of wanting and not having, of dreaming of Cole came crashing down to this one moment.

The details of her surroundings fell away as his hands brushed the jacket from her shoulders. She let the vintage Oleg Cassini piece drop to the floor where she stood.

She didn't want to need Cole. She didn't want to lust for the feel of him, the taste of him, the scent of him. But she lusted for him like she lusted for her next heartbeat. Her body screamed that if she didn't have him, she would die on the spot.

His touch prickled every nerve ending. He was so familiar yet so changed. Against her pale skin his hands looked big and capable, the hands of a surgeon.

And his body, once promising the potential of solid muscularity, now fulfilled that promise and more.

Closing her eyes, she breathed in. Yes, his scent after all these years was still the same yet more so, intoxicating with an undernote of confidence and success.

If she could stop herself from wanting him, she would.

That deep, dark look in his eyes told her he knew what she was thinking.

"Bella, let me show you what you've missed all these years."

As if drawn together by forces out of her control, she obeyed, leaning toward him. She stood on tiptoe, meeting his hungry, greedy mouth with her own.

His taste was so much more than her memories had promised. Or maybe it was her, now mature enough to indulge and savor.

Using her kiss, she showed him all the frustration she'd been living with for the last fourteen years.

With a lapse of control she'd never experienced before, she ripped his shirt open, resenting anything between them, literally as well as figuratively.

Grabbing the open edges of his shirt in her fists, she held him captive. "How badly do you want me?"

He took full advantage and pulled her to him, letting her feel his own need. "More than I can say."

"Then show me." She ran her hands down his pants. "Take them off."

Faster than she could react, he obliged, stripping off to bare skin.

Stunned—awed—she sucked in her breath at the magnificence of him. Her dreams of yesteryear were mere wispy shadows compared to the flesh-and-blood man before her.

"You, too." Without waiting for her cooperation, he pulled her camisole over her head and unzipped her skirt. She stepped out of it, standing before him in bra, matching bikini panties and very high heels. She was more beautiful than he'd even dreamed about.

"The hair…" His voice broke as if he were in his teens again.

She pulled the clip and shook her head, feeling wild and sexy as the tousled mass sprang free then floated onto her shoulders and down her back.

He reached out to touch, but she backed away.

"Not yet." She reached back to unhook her bra, fully aware her actions made her breasts peak.

"Slow down. I want to—"

"No. Next time." She brushed his hands away then stepped out of her lace panties and kicked off her shoes.

A wave of chilly shyness brushed over her, pebbling her skin. But Cole ran his hands over her, warming her with his caress. "I've never touched such beauty before."

He circled each of her nipples with his thumbs, making her catch her breath. Her own hands found his chest, echoing his motions. When he sucked in his own breath, she let her triumph emerge in her smile.

"Woman, you are such a temptress."

"The question is, how long will you withstand temptation? Or will I need to start without you?" She lay back on the pillows and ran her hand down her own stomach before crooking her finger at him to follow her down. "Are you coming?"

"I'm very, very close."

"How close?" She reached out for him.

He dodged, giving her a sadly sweet smile. "Wait. I have to protect you."

"You've learned a thing or two." She smiled back. "Hurry."

"All ready." On hands and knees, he held himself over her, teasing her. "Forgive me for taking this long?"

She stared up into his eyes, taking in the deeper meaning behind his answer.

"You're forgiven," she said, surprising herself when she answered his flippant question with heartfelt depth. This was the beginning of forgiving him for so much more.

Immediately, her desire for him went up several notches, higher than she'd thought possible.

The light cast by the bedside lamp made the muscles of his abdomen stand out in bas-relief. She ran her fingertip along the center line, all the way down, looking up at him in victory when he visibly caught his breath.

Total joy welled up inside her at her power. "You've convinced me. You want me."

His voice was rough and husky when he said, "I've never needed you more deeply."

This is so much more than sex. Bella pushed the candid thought away as she pulled Cole down to her and wrapped her legs around his hips. Time for reflection later.

Gone was the tenderness of their youth. Gone was the exploration. Here was raw emotion. *Years and years of it.*

Years of invisible injury seeking a cure, years of emptiness seeking to be filled.

She thrust and he met her, equals in every way. She reveled in the power between them.

They came together, over and over and over, each seeking release that only the other could give.

Until at last they lay spent. Bella draped herself across his sweating form as both their chests heaved, dragging in air as if they'd been denied it for way too long.

Cole watched Bella sleep, her eyes in REM. Was she dreaming of him?

He had been such a fool. Pride had kept him away from this fascinating woman and the child she'd borne him. *The arrogant stupidity of youth.*

An arcing pain raced from his neck through his shoulder. His left hand felt thick and numb.

He shifted, regretting that he had to disturb Bella to ease his pain.

No matter how hard to tried to rationalize it, he had a really bad feeling about the possible diagnosis.

Every time Cole had a shooting pain he remembered the night he'd been pinned under the rigging of his family's capsized shrimping boat, straining to hear signs of life from his mother, father or brother.

Could it be that his old injury, the one that had healed so quickly in his youthful past, now had consequences that would affect his future? His profession defined him. Without surgery, who was he? *Just a kid from the wrong side of town, looking for the meaning of existence.*

The mental pain outweighed the physical pain ten times over. But ignoring the problem wasn't making it go away. He had put off a diagnosis for too long, hoping it would get better on its own—but neither wishing nor hoping was working.

Bella opened her eyes and looked into his face. "I hope that scowl isn't for me."

"No. Only kisses for you." He brushed his lips against the worried furrows of her forehead.

Then the silence between them stretched into awkwardness, underscoring how far apart they had drifted despite their present physical closeness.

Bella pulled the sheets up to her neck. "I know this sounds odd after what we've just done."

"You mean after wild, passionate lovemaking?"

"And a round of True Confessions." She gave him a lopsided smile. "But I feel rather shy about being completely naked in front of you. Would you mind closing your eyes while I snatch my clothes and duck into the bathroom?"

"Anything for you."

She sat up and looked across the hotel suite and his gaze followed hers. "What a mess I've made."

He'd never seen a room as sexy as this one, with her clothes scattered in reckless abandon. "I like it."

"I need to borrow your brush. My hair is a mess." She put her hand to her mussed hair then to her cheek. "And my makeup—surely Adrian will be asleep when I get home. But David will notice. How wrinkled is my jacket?"

Cole followed her on her frantic flight, catching her in front of the bathroom mirror. He saved her from herself and stopped her nervous babbling with his mouth on hers. When he let her come up for air, he looked down at her swollen lips, her dazed eyes, her mussed hair. He'd never seen a woman more beautiful. Seeing the image of the two of them together made him want to hold her for ever.

"Don't go." He hadn't realized he'd said it out loud until he heard his own voice. He'd never spent the entire night with a woman. Usually, he insisted on going out for a midnight snack, and then escorted them back to their own rooms. To the more determined ones, he just said no.

But Bella was different.

"Stay." He gave her his most charming smile. "Please?"

He watched the indecision play across her eyes. Finally, she blinked and looked at him. "Okay."

As if he'd been holding his breath for the last decade and a half, he exhaled.

"Thank you." He brushed an errant strand of hair from her cheek. In the filtered light the smudges under her eyes showed the weariness her life must bring her.

Holding her hand as if she would bolt, he led her back to bed. "I want you but you need sleep."

"And you don't?" She asked the rhetorical question. She could always read him. "You look like you're carrying the weight of the world on your shoulders."

Her words made him feel exposed. "Let me get the bathroom light."

He slipped from the covers to turn off the light.

While he was up, he heard her reach for the phone.

"How's our boy?" She must be calling David.

Cole winced at all the years David had claimed his son. Despite his lassitude, anger at himself flared to life, quickly followed by guilt. Because of pride, because of rage, he had missed so much. Grudgingly, he couldn't help but be grateful Adrian had someone to care for him. And there was no going back in time, no fixing past regrets.

"If you can watch him through the night, I want to stay."

What would David say to that? Cole couldn't imagine his answer. But whatever it was, it must have been positive, because Bella answered with, "Thank you, and I will."

He hovered his hand over his prescription pain medication and chose aspirin instead. He didn't want to be fuzzy-headed in the morning, when he would awaken to see Bella in first light.

When he heard the phone clatter on the bedside table, Cole made his appearance.

He climbed into bed, enjoying Bella's sweet, cold toes raking down his leg. He had once promised always to keep her feet warm. He would finally get to fulfill that promise.

At least for tonight. Always seemed like a long way away.

She placed a featherlight kiss on the juncture between his neck and shoulder where he hurt the worst. Did she know?

"I'm sorry, Bella. I should have—"

"Shh." She put her finger against his lips. "If we had stayed together then, where would we be now? Would I still be that clinging girl afraid to carve out my own place in the world, resenting you because of it? Would you have even finished school? I know you think so, but you had such pride. You couldn't have afforded a wife, a special-needs baby and medical school on a part-time job. Admit it, Cole. Leaving me felt like leaving an anchor behind, didn't it?"

He watched the shadows flicker across the ceiling. "Yes, it did, but not like you think. You were my anchor, the one person who grounded me and kept me sane. You were my reason to be steady and stay the course toward my goal. Without you, I was adrift, just like I was after my parents drowned."

When he found himself rubbing at his hand, he reached

for Bella's instead. "When I left you behind to go to New York, I have never felt so alone, not even after the funerals."

"Even if you had stayed, it might not have worked. Maybe deep down I knew that. Maybe that's why I didn't go after you. Who knows?" Bella reached with her free hand and guided his face to look into hers. "Recriminations do neither of us any good. We were young and foolish and impetuous. We can't go back in time. What's done is done."

"I was impetuous. You were cautious. I led where you weren't ready to go."

"You led me into the vast brightness of the world when I would have stayed safely hidden in the gray shadows of my father's house. You showed me a depth of passion and excitement and joy I would have never discovered without you."

"I hurt you, too."

"As I hurt you." She rubbed her finger along his eyebrow, smoothing out the tension. "I've already begun to heal."

"I'm glad." If only he hadn't been the one to inflict that pain, so much would be different between them right now. He was grateful Bella had offered him absolution but it didn't change anything. Some men weren't made to have a family and he had proof, twice over, that he was one of those men. He'd made peace with that a long time ago and was content with his solitary state.

He would steal a few more days from his work and make arrangements so that Bella and Adrian would never want for anything again. Then he would go back to his practice, the one thing in life he had to offer the world, with the small comfort that he had done what he could to correct his past. It was for the best for everyone.

Isabella tugged at the blanket pinned beneath him. "Is it getting chilly in here?"

He thought about promising to keep her warm, but he'd

already promised to let her sleep—and his thoughts on body heat had nothing to do with rest.

He rose up and covered her silky shoulder with the blanket, giving in to temptation and gliding his hand along that graceful curve.

"Good night," she said, before turning onto her side with her back to him.

"Good night, Bella," he whispered in her ear.

A sweet lassitude settled in his soul as she settled into her pillow, curving her body into a C, her bare derrière brushing his naked stomach. He wrapped himself around her, wanting her yet knowing next time he could go slowly and savor his time with her.

As he drifted to sleep, he realized that was exactly what he had thought the last time they'd lain together.

Bella had thought she would have a hard time falling to sleep. She had expected to be keyed up and nervous, in bed with a man. The last time she'd shared a bed had been with this very same man—so different yet so much the same.

But Cole's arm around her, his body cradling hers, gave her a warmth and security to drift off into. Without a worry on her mind she fell into the most restful sleep she'd had in years.

As the bright sun pierced the gap between the curtains, Bella awoke alone.

Cole's pillow still held his impression. The sheets still held his scent. But the chill on her skin was no longer warmed from his heat.

She ran her tongue across her fuzzy teeth and decided to make the best of it. Was there any other option?

Yes, there was. Once she would have bolted in panic. But she was no longer that young, scared girl left in a lurch.

While she could sneak out, hoping she wouldn't run into

anyone she knew, her running and sneaking days were long past, along with her unconfident youth.

She was a woman grown now and she would never again let unanswered questions lie between them. She would practice patience, withhold judgment and wait for Cole to return, though the discipline of waiting patiently certainly tested her maturity.

With David taking Adrian to the jazz and blues festival, Isabella had a rare morning to herself and she intended to enjoy every minute of it.

Using Cole's toothpaste and her finger, she did the best she could, but the taste and feel of his mouth lingered in her memory. So did the memory of his hands, his strength and warmth, his on-the-edge restraint and her lack of the same.

In another time and place she would have been embarrassed about her unbridled passion. Right now, she was rather proud of herself.

Deliberately, she chose to enjoy a long, hot shower to soak out the soreness of unused muscles. After she'd soaped and rinsed every inch of skin, rubbing in Cole's touch rather than rubbing it off, she used his brush to untangle her hair.

No cosmetics. Despite the dark shadows under her eyes and a few squint lines at the corners, she had held up fairly well to single motherhood of a special-needs child.

What would her life be like now if she had gotten notice to Cole about the pregnancy, and he had married her out of duty?

The mirror fogged, revealing a finger-drawn message, a big heart with "I Love You" written across it for an earlier recipient. How many lovers had this room hosted?

Isabella smiled at the revealed artwork, but it was a sad, nostalgic smile. Once, maybe, she could have been that steamy graffiti artist. But now, even if she wanted to love that way, she'd learned too much caution to let it happen.

And she didn't have the time or the energy to convince herself otherwise.

Wrapping a large towel around her body, she opened the bathroom door. As the bathroom fog dissipated, so did the message in the mirror.

Cole, in running shorts and T-shirt, sat in a chair, scrolling through his phone messages. Sacks and two cups from one of the downstairs bakeries sat on the table next to him.

"I thought you might like—" He looked up and saw her standing there. Visibly, he swallowed, obviously at a loss for words.

His reaction inspired a boldness she hadn't even known she had.

Should she? It would be so unlike her.

Wasn't that what she needed? To break from her normal routine of mother and health-care professional? To be herself—the self she never let herself be? To live a little?

Need. That was the key emotion right now.

She unwrapped the towel. "I thought *you* might like…"

He dropped his cellphone and didn't bother to pick it up.

"Yes." He swallowed as he stood. "I like. Very much."

She studied him, head to toe. "You're overdressed."

In the next instant he wasn't.

This time Isabella enjoyed Cole's leisurely exploration as he touched her gently, reverently.

In the full light of day, standing toe to toe, he explored her body, caressing every inch. If she had any worries about flaws like her C-section scar, he kissed them away before they could make her feel uneasy.

She traced the whirl of hair across his chest, down to the flatness of his stomach. He followed the same route on her, his fingers splayed as his large palm covered her belly. Then he slid his hand lower. One flick of his finger and her knees refused to hold her any longer.

In total sync to her reaction, he caught her and carried her to the bed. Wrapping her arms around him, she pulled him down to cover her.

He broke contact only long enough to dash into the bathroom for a packet so he could protect her.

For an insane instant Bella wished it could be otherwise, wished she could have more of Cole's babies, wished they could be a family.

Then his mouth came down on hers and all she could think was how she wanted to give back, thrust for thrust.

This time they took their time, letting the urgency build as they both breathed in unison, faster and faster.

With a cry Bella let her emotions overcome her. Pleasure flooded through her as Cole pulsed within her.

Together.

It felt so right.

Instead of sweet lethargy, Bella felt a surge of refreshing vitality. Look out world, here comes Bella!

As her fingers traced patterns in the sweat on Cole's stomach, he said, "I've got today free. Want to play tourist with me?"

With Cole's invitation, the outside world intruded.

What had she done?

A panicked, suffocating, frantic reaction started in her stomach, growing and growing until it reached her brain.

"No," she forced out, trying to keep from hyperventilating.

She rolled out of bed, scooped up her cold, damp towel and wrapped it around her.

Awkward didn't begin to describe how she felt holding up her towel while bending down to grab yesterday's skirt and jacket, camisole and bra from across a hotel suite that suddenly seemed as vast and as open as the Ponchartrain.

Catching a glimpse of Cole's bewildered face as she rushed

past him for the safety of the bathroom only increased her manic mood.

"Bella?" Cole knocked on the door. "Are you okay in there?"

"Fine. Just fine." She was fully aware that her shrill, hysteria-tinged voice sounded anything but fine as she realized she hadn't gathered up her panties in her mad dash.

"Do you need these?"

Isabella stood behind the door, opened it just enough to hold out her hand, and felt the hard edges of her shoe heels carefully balanced across her open palm.

Not what she was expecting, but strangely comforting to think that Cole must understand her need to flee. Either that, or he wanted the emotional one-night stand out of his room as much as she wanted to go.

As her initial burst of panicked adrenaline leveled off, embarrassment took its place. She had never been a drama queen before. But she'd never been wanton and wild before either. Cole brought out an unrestrained side of her that made her feel free to follow her impulses. Which couldn't be a good thing when she had so much responsibility to juggle, could it?

Once dressed, she took hold of herself. Avoiding the mirror to avoid the wild-eyed, crazy woman she knew she would see there, she straightened her spine.

She would exit with dignity if it was the last thing she ever did, even if she could feel the breeze all too well on her bare bottom.

Isabella took a deep breath and opened the door.

Cole sat in the same chair as he had earlier, wearing the same shorts he had worn. He looked up with the same questioning gaze.

If only she could go back in time.

No—that was not what she wanted. Her time with Cole

was a gift she would not regret. But she needed to get control of herself and move on.

She looked past him toward the door. "My purse. I can't remember where I put it."

He pointed to the coffee table behind him where her purse lay on its side with the contents spilled across the table. He had laid her panties between her cellphone and her keys.

Knowing that he knew she was bare-bottomed made her twitch despite her resolve.

"This is not how we end this, Bella." He stood. Anger sparked in his eyes. So he hadn't forgiven her yet. Even more reason for putting space between them.

"Far from it. This is only the beginning."

Bella's face was a mask, calm, polite—cold. If he hadn't been watching so intently, he wouldn't have seen the quaver at the corner of her mouth or the worry in her crystal eyes.

"Cole—"

He held up his hand, stopping her. "I intend to take care of my son, make financial arrangements for him and for you."

The intention to take care of Bella made Cole feel as if the pieces of his world, shattered all those years ago, were finally falling into place.

Her nod was brisk, a sharp movement of acknowledgment just shy of acceptance. "I'll call you. Right now I need some breathing room."

From an intellectual perspective, he understood—but he was a man of action. Sitting around waiting for Bella to think through her emotions would be a lesson in patience he would rather do without.

"Soon, Bella. Make it soon."

"It's been fifteen years. A few more—"

"Hours? Days? Years? I've missed so much already." He stopped himself. How much involvement did he want, other than having his accountant make deposits each month?

He had a son, a part of himself. Then there was Isabella. Could he cut her out of his life now that he had found her once again?

"Soon." She walked around him, shoveled her things into her purse, tucking her panties down deep, and walked toward the door.

He shook his head to clear it. His profession was all he needed. And neither Bella nor Adrian needed him beyond financial help. She had become too strong of a woman to be dependent on any man. The sooner he left New Orleans the sooner he could leave behind the edginess that clouded his thinking.

Just when he thought she would leave him without another word, she turned to face him. "Welcome home, Cole."

Home. The hotel room mocked the sentiment behind the word.

Home to him meant family and he hadn't had a family since his teens.

But now he did. He had a son.

For the first time in a very long time uncertainty took away all his answers.

CHAPTER SEVEN

WHEN David had brought Adrian home from the jazz festival, she had been barely coherent when she'd said she didn't want to talk about it. She owed him a big thank-you, as well as an apology for being so abrupt.

Putting a few hours between her and Cole had been of no help as Isabella tried to figure out what last night—and this morning—meant to her. She hadn't even gotten to the repercussion part of her actions. And then there was the mind shift that Cole hadn't known about Adrian all these years.

Still in a daze, she now went through the motions of dining with her father and her son. All three of them looked forward to the two nights a week when she and Adrian picked him up from the nursing home and took him for an outing.

"You're quiet tonight, daughter." Her father struggled to string the words together despite the years of speech therapy that had followed his stroke. Some days were better than others.

He sat in his chair with as much dignity as his shrunken body would allow him. He may have lost his health but he hadn't lost his intelligence—although the world often treated him as if his mind was as feeble as his body. She was as guilty as the rest.

Tonight she'd almost done the unthinkable and canceled their outing, but her father's encroaching weakness, and the twinkle in his eyes whenever she and Adrian visited, made her treasure every moment spent with him. So she had dug down for her last half-gallon of strength, and here they sat.

She looked at her dear papa, who had always done his best by her, even when he'd been totally bewildered about how to raise a daughter.

"I'm just tired. I've been juggling a lot this week." The dark circles under her eyes were visible proof that she needed a rest.

Usually, she tried to carry a conversation, if for no other reason than to keep herself from having to eat in silence. His life in the nursing home tended to have as little excitement as hers. She would normally be regaling him with stories about the hospital, a life he missed desperately, but she was doing all she could to keep up the pretense of eating. She had nothing leftover within her to play the role of gracious hostess.

As soon as the waiter cleared the table of dishes and set down the traditional two cups of coffee and cup of hot chocolate, Adrian pulled his doctor doll from his backpack.

She continually wondered what went on in her son's head but tonight she didn't have to guess as Adrian held the doll in front of his grandfather's face, trying his best to communicate that his own personal superhero was in town.

"What's this, Adrian?" her father directed the question to his grandson, but expected the answer from her.

"It's a long story." Isabella hesitated about how much to tell him. "Sorry to be such bad company. I've got a lot on my mind." By the time she got her head together she might owe everyone in New Orleans her sincerest apologies for her lapse in manners.

"Can I help?" He lifted his hands and let them fall onto the armrests of his wheelchair. "I can't do much, but I can listen."

"Thanks, Papa. Maybe later." She wanted to shelter him from worry, but she did desperately needed someone to talk to. Not for the first time lately she vowed she would make time to develop girlfriend friendships—as soon as she figured out how to stretch a normal twenty-four-hour day.

His concerned eyes glossed over with sadness. "Whenever you're ready."

Just as defeat started to color his eyes, she reached over and put her hand on his. "Cole Lassiter is back in town and I'm not sure what to do about it. I know we really never talked about it, you and I. But he never came back because he saw the engagement announcement and thought I'd made my choice over him."

Her father blinked, the cloudiness clearing from his eyes. "I always wondered. I should have asked."

She had to pick her words very carefully, with Adrian sitting there. As her son stared out the window, he could be taking in every word—or not comprehending any of it.

But Isabella had never really affirmed to anyone other than David that Cole was Adrian's father. Now she felt compelled to. Even though the truth had lain dormant all these years, it now felt like a lie of omission to let anyone think otherwise.

For shining a light on her secret, she would hate Cole right now if she could figure out how. But hate was the one emotion she didn't feel for Cole. She felt lust, security, lo— No, not that emotion. That was just leftover infatuation, even if it felt totally different.

Under her hand, her father's fingers twitched. She turned her attention back to her confession.

"I sent letters and he says he tore them up before reading them and he didn't know about..." She cast a sideways glance at Adrian. "And I believe him. At least my head does. My heart doesn't know what to believe."

Her father's eyes reflected alarm as well as concern.

He paused, gathering his words.

"I must ask your forgiveness, Isabella."

"Why, Papa?"

"I was weak where I should have been strong. I let Mrs. Beautemps take over when I didn't have the heart to face my responsibilities. Your mother was such a good parent, making all the decisions, doing all the planning, bringing all the joy to our household. I never learned to live without her. Because of that, I failed you." He gasped as if he had run out of air as well as out of words.

"No, Papa. Don't say that."

"You've been a good parent, Isabella, like your mother. But Adrian needs all the love he can get—and, Isabella, so do you."

Emotion spilled from the eyes that used to be so stoic. He reached for his napkin but his gnarled hand couldn't grasp the flimsy paper. As Isabella wiped his face for him, he touched her wrist. "I am sorry to be such a burden."

"You're not a burden, Papa. You're my family." Emotional overload had her pushing her chair away from the table on the pretense of going to the ladies' room. "I'll be right back."

At the register, Isabella asked for the bill, knowing how much her father regretted having to rely on his daughter to pay his way. He may have been an excellent doctor, but he was a horrible money manager, as Isabella had discovered in the days following his stroke.

She dug through her purse for the familiar feel of her wallet, wincing every time she touched the panties she had forgotten to remove earlier.

After too many minutes of fruitless foraging, she had to accept her first fear. Her wallet had fallen out in Cole's room.

The cashier narrowed her eyes in suspicion. "There's no problem, is there?"

Isabella gave the woman a reassuring smile. "I have to make a phone call."

She stepped away into the foyer with Cole's card in her

hand. When she had taken it from Adrian's room, telling him he needed to let her know before he made a call, she had felt awkward, but now she was glad she had the tattered and bent card.

Cole answered on the second ring. "Adrian?"

She swallowed twice, trying to find her voice.

"I'm glad you called, son." His voice sounded thick and emotional.

"Sorry to disappoint you but it's not Adrian. It's me—Isabella."

"Yes?" This time he sounded cautious, as if expecting anything.

"I'm in a bit of a fix. When I spilled my purse, I think my wallet must have fallen under the coffee table."

"Hold on. I'll check." After a moment of rustling noises, Cole came back on the line. "I have it here."

"Could you bring it to me? I'm at Merci Beau Coup."

"Yes, I can do that."

"Thanks." She looked toward her table where Adrian was again trying to hand his doctor doll to his grandfather. "And, Cole, could you just drop it off with the hostess? I'm…" How could she put this best? "I'm not alone."

That probably wasn't the best way, but her brain cells weren't working at full speed right now.

"You're asking me to stay out of sight around your friends? This sounds like old times, Isabella."

"No, it's not like that." Isabella flushed, realizing how loudly she had spoken in such a public place. She lowered her voice. "I'm with my dad and he's not very healthy. I don't want to shock him."

"I may not have been raised with your fancy manners, but I had no intention of bursting into the restaurant and announcing to all and sundry that we made love all night and all morning."

The memory of those sweet lovemaking sessions warmed Isabella in so many places.

"Just bring the wallet, Cole."

"Princess, your wish is my command." The sound of the line going dead in her ear spoke a message louder than all the other noises around her.

A quick glance toward her table showed Adrian building a bridge with his French fries and her father slowly sipping his coffee. She would make a quick trip to the ladies' room to compose herself before she rejoined her family.

But when she came out, she found Cole waiting for her.

He held out her wallet. "I've settled your bill."

She reached for it, feeling like a charity recipient. "I'm not destitute."

His hand brushed hers as she took the wallet from him. She jerked away as if he'd burned her. Why had she given in to that spark inside her? She should have known better than to play with fire.

"I'm making up for lost time. I should have been supporting you and Adrian for the last decade and a half. Consider it my first installment."

From the corner of her eye she saw that Adrian had spotted Cole and was making his way toward them. "You've got to go."

Cole turned to follow her line of vision. "Is that your father with Adrian?"

She nodded.

"When are you going to introduce me to your father?"

"When I'm ready."

"It seems like I've heard that before—fifteen years ago, Bella." He crossed his arms and gave her an uncompromising stare. "I don't hide my relationships. I'm not that kind of man."

They both watched as Adrian bumped chairs and waiters to get to Cole.

"Papa and I have just discussed my past—our past—and it's still raw. Cole, please…" The last time she'd begged him had been in bed that morning. She had been ecstatic when he'd accommodated her then.

"Please, what?" By the way he arched his brow, she knew he remembered just as she did.

"That has nothing to do with this." Her bravado failed her. She hugged herself, feeling totally vulnerable and alone. "Just go."

Cole's eyes flashed. "You won't keep me away from my son." He softened it with, "I'll say hello to your father as one professional to another. It's respectful."

Professional courtesy would mean so much to her father. How could Cole know all her weak spots?

Twenty feet away, Adrian made a desperate twist and turn round the hostess who was seating a party of six to get to Cole.

Once he had closed the gap, he held out a bread basket. "Pigeons."

A new word. Isabella struggled to keep her emotions in check. Her son was having a breakthrough, saying things and doing things he'd never done before. Isabella couldn't ignore that Adrian's progress had coincided with Cole's appearance.

Cole took the basket his son shoved at him. "Pigeons?"

Adrian looked at his mother, his hand flapping in frustration.

Isabella smiled through the tears welling in her eyes. "We always walk to Jackson Square and feed the pigeons after we eat here. It's a tradition."

"I could do with a walk. Besides, I've broken enough of your traditions recently."

At that, Adrian rushed back to the table, unlocked his

grandfather's wheelchair, and ever so carefully pushed it through the throngs of diners.

Cole held out his hand. "Dr. Allante, it is an honor to finally meet you."

"Likewise. My grandson seems to be very fond of you."

"We met when I volunteered at the special games." How easily could that meeting have never happened. Even though he'd only known of Adrian for such a short time, he couldn't imagine his son not being in his life.

Apparently, Adrian decided they'd had enough time for the social niceties as he started pushing his grandfather's wheelchair toward the door.

He looked over his shoulder, giving Cole and Isabella a look that clearly said, Come on.

The hostess hurried toward them, carrying a paper sack. "Adrian, wait. Stale bread, with our compliments. For our favorite patron."

Bella held her breath, waiting for Adrian to snatch the bag and bolt. He wasn't very good at being approached by strangers. Her apologies were ready on the tip of her tongue.

Instead, Adrian gave a sideways look toward Cole as if to say, See how they like me? Then he gave a polite nod to the hostess, snagged the bag and dropped it into his grandfather's saddlebag.

Another breakthrough, as he showed off for his father. How could Cole just waltz into their lives and make such a huge difference in so short a time? What would happen when he left?

She wasn't just thinking of Adrian's reaction either.

Walking through the French Quarter, Cole couldn't help but be proud of the woman next to him, who turned the heads of all the other men. He knew it was superficial to feel boastful about having the best-looking woman in New Orleans on his arm, but there was only so much natural inclination a man should have to suppress.

How could she make a simple T-shirt, khaki shorts and sandals look so sexy? In his own casual shorts, T-shirt and tennis shoes, he felt like part of a couple, complete and whole with his other half at his side. He felt like he belonged. It was a good feeling, a fifteen-year-old feeling, one he had never felt with any other woman except the one at his side.

Ahead of him, his son—his son!—pushed Bella's father. On the outside, it was a picture-perfect outing. But inside there was still so much to resolve. Complications abounded instead of the closure he'd hoped to find here.

Cole took a deep breath, trying to inhale it all. The sights, sounds and scents of New Orleans were like no other place in the world. Brine and humidity so thick it felt like a steam room. Splashes of color in flower boxes, on doors and in clothes. The cacophony of different languages, thick with accents, blending together to create an energy that exactly meshed with his own.

For all the years he'd called home the concrete, glass and neon of New York City, he had thought of New Orleans as a city of painful memories. Being back was a bittersweet homecoming.

And the beautiful woman next to him was responsible for a large share of the bitter as well as most of the sweet. Having Bella by his side made him temporarily forget all those old hurts—hurts she herself had inflicted.

That Bella had tried to smooth it all over by saying his not knowing had worked out for the best only fueled his fire.

Painful emotions crashed over him. Rejection of the boy from the wrong neighborhood. Betrayal with David. Missed years with his son.

Rage raced through him, rage and guilt. If he had only opened one of her letters, listened to one of her voicemails, he would have been taking care of his responsibilities all these years instead of being forever in Isabella's and Adrian's debt.

He could have made life better for her and for Adrian. Or maybe not. Bella was right. He'd had nothing to offer back then. And now?

What did he have that Bella or Adrian would want or need, other than money?

Bella must have sensed his change of mood—she always had—because she moved away on the pretense of inspecting a sidewalk artist's abstract rendition of the Gulf of Mexico with a tropical storm approaching. Her face was still, a mask devoid of emotion—so different than the passion she showed him in bed.

The emotional distance she put between them felt wider than the physical distance.

"What are you thinking?" he asked, attempting to bridge the crevasse of silence.

She gave him a long look, as if she were trying to see inside his head—or his soul. "I like this one. All that energy about to be unleashed feels so powerful."

Shrugging off her scrutiny, he said, "I would have guessed you preferred more formal, reserved work." He gestured to the landscape in oils. The classic painting of a white-columned plantation home had a manicured lawn with mossy live oak trees in the foreground. "Proper and predictable."

She gave him a sideways look as she took a step away. "I've been misjudged by a lot of people, Cole Lassiter. Don't make the same mistake."

Cole wanted to ask about the wistfulness in her eyes, but he had pushed too hard for now.

Instead, he gestured toward Adrian, who had stopped amid the fortune-tellers, artists and street performers in front of St. Louis Cathedral and locked his grandfather's chair. The two of them were taking their time doling out the stale bread as they enjoyed each other's companionship. Cole envied their closeness. "We might be here a while. Want to sit?"

"As long as I can keep an eye on them." She held up her hand, shading her eyes and inadvertently showing off her small waist.

Last night, he had traced every inch of her perfect body, felt the hum of her excitement surround him and vibrate through him until he'd felt electric, charged—like the impending storm in the painting.

He had the urgent yearning to feel the life force that was so uniquely Bella. After their night together, a casual touch shouldn't be a big deal. But Bella had pulled herself back with such reserve, Cole deliberated before breaching her barriers.

As he guided her to an empty bench a few yards away, Cole took a chance and rested his hand on the small of her back. His risk was rewarded when she didn't pull away.

What was this energy between them? Nostalgia? Rekindled attraction? A whole new allure that had nothing to do with their past?

Was Bella as confused about this thing between them as he was?

The sounds of the Mississippi River, of ships and boats of every size and description, blended with a saxophonist's song as he brought up music from his soul, hoping for spare change.

Bella breathed in the beautiful early evening and the joy of having her family at peace as the symphony of life played around her. These were the precious moments, the ones she worked so hard to preserve. Cole brought a different note to her song, but not a discordant one.

Adrian waved his hand at the pigeons, making them all fly. They settled back quickly enough, hoping he had dropped crumbs in his mad dash.

Nothing brought a smile to Adrian's face like feeding these birds with his grandfather.

When Adrian smiled, Bella's world lit up.

Cole's smile affected her the same way. That had been her reaction from the start, all those years ago.

Sadly, both smiles were rare.

Adrian was growing up in so many ways yet still a child in so many others. What would happen to her son beyond her lifetime? What if she became ill? Who would take care of her child then? It was a worry parents of all special-needs children had—a worry they could never assuage.

Her sigh came from deep within before she could hold it back.

"Long night?" Cole's deep voice rumbled in the same sexy way he'd whispered in her ear when they'd lain together after making love.

A delicious shiver went through her. She reminded herself that he would be on his way back to New York in the next day or two.

"So much has happened in the last twenty-four hours. Seeing you again, learning you'd never received my letters about Adrian, sleeping with you when I haven't been with a man since—"

"Since when? Since David?"

She grinned at his bristling curiosity. "A lady doesn't kiss and tell. Let's just leave that one unsaid, okay?" That she and David had never consummated their marriage wasn't just her secret but David's also.

She thought of all the women Cole's name had been linked with. Not that it mattered. Last night had definitely been a one-night stand. This whole weekend seemed like a slice of unreality in her otherwise stable life. The surreal chaos would soon be over so she could go on with the orderly lifestyle she worked so hard to maintain.

She was glad of that. Wasn't she?

"I'm setting up a trust fund for Adrian."

The pride and independence Isabella had worked toward for so long warred with practicality.

At her hesitation, Cole added, "It's my responsibility and my privilege. I insist on being part of his financial future and I will be contributing to his everyday expenses, too. He's my son."

While Cole's abandonment of her had cut her to the bone, his paternity had been nothing more than an empty fact.

Now, on a deeper level, she acknowledged Adrian was Cole's son as well as hers. "Yes, he is your son. Thank you."

The admission felt like she was loosening her grip on her claim to parenthood. It was uncomfortable yet so very freeing to know she no longer carried the whole burden alone.

Her mind took a flight of fantasy. What would it be like to share day-to-day parenting with Cole? To share the bed with Cole every night? Never to be alone again?

Live in the moment, Bella, she told herself. Planning for an uncertain future is letting your dreams run away with your logic.

Still, it was nice sitting here with their shoulders touching and Cole's warmth seeping into her. She wished this moment could last forever.

Just for the moment she would indulge in the fantasy that it could.

CHAPTER EIGHT

BELLA'S stillness unnerved Cole, making him yearn for action—like picking her up, throwing her over his shoulder, carrying her off to the nearest cave and not coming out for a week. But then what?

Uncertainty worked its wicked knife into Cole's future, ripping to shreds all his plans of putting his past behind him.

One thing he knew without a doubt. As long as New Orleans held Bella and Adrian, it held a piece of him as well.

Around him, the world buzzed with movement. The exotic atmosphere of his home city was like no other in the world. He had been so anxious to escape all this.

A shrimp boat chugged by, the odor of diesel mixing with all New Orleans' other scents. He couldn't make out the crew on board but could too easily imagine a family of father, mother and two overgrown boys coming in with the day's catch.

"Stop." Bella put her hand over his clenched fist, startling him from his imaginings. "Whatever you're thinking about right now, stop. You're giving yourself pain."

Cole opened his palm, hoping Bella would leave her hand in his. But she withdrew it, lacing her fingers together in her lap, clearly regretting reaching out to him.

"Sorry. It's really none of my business how you choose to feel, is it?"

"Is this what you do? Is this kind of analysis part of your practice?"

Distracted, she looked past him. "With Adrian, I can't turn it off. I have to always be on the alert to his smallest nuance. I love my son from head to toe. But always being aware of his every movement, adjusting my behavior to moderate his, assessing his slightest reactions so I can understand his needs, has become ingrained with me."

"It must be exhausting."

Bella cocked her head sideways. "I see it in other parents' faces. I've often wondered if they see it on mine. But I've been doing it for so long I can't imagine my life without having to be tuned in all the time."

Cole soon saw what had distracted Bella. A family of five, mom, dad and three children spread out in age. The oldest boy had a medal around his neck Cole recognized from the special games. He showed the physical characteristics of Down's syndrome. A toddler rode on her mother's hip while Dad pushed a baby in a stroller. The parents looked like they were desperately seeking holiday happiness but not quite finding it.

"I want to be involved in my son's life."

Myriad emotions crossed Bella's face. Rebellion. Anger. Confusion. And resignation. "Give me your email address in New York and I'll email you regularly."

At this moment, he couldn't even think about returning to New York. All he could thing about was being here, now, with Bella only a breath away from him.

What would Bella think if he leaned over and kissed away the tightness around her mouth? But he knew that would be moving too fast for her.

Honesty time. They were moving too fast for *him*.

He had always had a vision for his future, knowing his next goal, planning his next step. But a fourteen-year-old boy had never fit into that plan.

"I intend to fly in and visit as often as I can." Decision made, he felt in control of his world once again.

Cole didn't have to be a behavioral therapist to read Bella's cautious body language. "That won't work. Adrian needs routine. He doesn't respond well to change."

"The only constant in life is change."

"Did you read that in a fortune cookie?"

Cole caught himself tensing his shoulders. Pain radiated through his back, up his neck and along his skull.

Deliberately, he took a breath and leaned back on the bench. "I would never do anything to hurt Adrian or you."

"Cole, you don't understand. Any child would have trouble adjusting to a parent dropping in and out of his life, but Adrian is special. As hard as both Adrian and I work to make him fit in, there are some aspects of his life that just don't work like other people's. He needs consistency. Unless you're planning on moving back to New Orleans, you becoming involved in Adrian's life won't be good for him." Her eyes froze like glaciers. "But, then, that was one of your goals, wasn't it? To leave all this behind."

His mouth twisted in a crooked grimace. "That was the plan."

As if the glaciers had melted as quickly as they'd frozen, her eyes became soft and watery. How deeply had she been hurt by his rejection? At least as deeply as he had ached when he'd crumpled her engagement announcement in his fist.

Bella grabbed his hands, squeezing them between her own small palms. "Why, Cole? Why did you always want to leave?"

She didn't understand. How could she when he'd never told her?

Where most people found calm in the water rolling past, Cole found anxiousness. The power of the waves lapping the shore made from the wakes of the slow-moving barges aggravated a restlessness deep inside him.

As always when he thought of that day, he felt vestiges of that night, heard the water slap the side of their wrecked shrimp boat, heard the sounds of his brother's whimpering getting weaker with each inch of movement of the sun toward the horizon.

Why now? Why, when he normally forced his mind to skirt past those memories, was he willingly allowing them to flow?

The answer was in the small, delicate hand clasped in his. Isabella brought him a security he found nowhere else. That was how it had been from the moment they had first brushed fingertips all those years ago.

"My father loved the water. My mother tolerated it, because my father loved it."

"She loved him very deeply."

"Yes."

Remembering Bella's advice, Cole deliberately relaxed his neck and jaw. "My brother was just like my father. He wanted to follow in Dad's footsteps."

"But you?"

"I was always worried I would be trapped in shrimping. My father had worked hard to build up a family business to pass on to his sons. He wanted to leave us with a legacy."

Cole thought hard, trying to remember what his father had looked like. He remembered feelings, impressions, but the visual memories were fuzzy. "My dad wasn't even fifty, but he was already thinking of our future."

"But it wasn't the future you wanted. Did he know that?"

"No. As hard as he worked for us, I didn't want to disappoint him by telling him I didn't want to spend my life on a boat." The knot at the base of Cole's neck throbbed and threatened to cramp. He could stop, change the subject, walk away from the pain.

"I knew there was a boating accident, but you never told me what happened. Tell me, Cole. Tell me the rest of it."

"Nothing but truth between us..." Cole looked out at the water, unwilling to see the condemnation in Bella's eyes. "It could have been my fault."

"The wreck?"

"Yes. A tropical storm was blowing in. I was supposed to keep an eye on the weather and let my dad know how fast it was moving. Money was tight—it was always tight. Shrimping is always poor right after a storm brings in a cold front, so we needed to stay on the water as long as we could before the weather changed."

"That's a lot of responsibility for a young boy."

"Not so young. I was thirteen, and I had been born into the business, remember? I knew what I was supposed to do."

For the first time in all these years Cole forced himself to think back. "I had part of my attention on the weather forecast, but the other part was in the book I was reading. I was always getting into trouble for not paying attention to details—I guess I'm guilty of the same thing getting you pregnant with Adrian."

"It takes two. I don't recall protesting." Bella squeezed his hand. "And I would never trade having Adrian for a chance to do it over."

The sincerity in Bella's voice convinced him she was being totally truthful. Her response eased the guilt he'd felt ever since he'd found out he'd walked out on his pregnant girl-friend.

"Cole, what happened that day?"

Could Bella absolve him of this guilt, too? "I remember wanting to go in to shore. The Gulf has a different feel, a different rhythm right before a storm."

Cole could still remember the color of the water, the smell in the air, all different with the approaching storm. Nature's warning system, his father had said.

"But one of the nets snagged. We couldn't afford to lose a net so we were trying to pull it in, but the wind picked up."

His throat ached. He realized he'd stopped talking and was staring out into the mouth of the Gulf. Bile rose as he remembered.

"Finally, Dad said to leave it and we cut it loose." He remembered the feel of the bulky knife in his hands as he sawed through the ropes that represented a large portion of his family's livelihood.

"Mom was already steering us home, with us dragging that net. I could see the storm coming, a dark solid blackness of water punctuated by lightning. The winds picked up, throwing us from side to side."

Cole blinked, surprised to find the day was bright and cheerful around him. "I remember waking up, trapped under debris. My brother was close enough to touch. He was making a low whimpering sound. My father kept telling my mother over and over again he was sorry. The next time I regained consciousness the Coastguard was lifting me onto their boat. I was the only survivor."

"I'm so sorry, Cole." Tears tracked down Bella's face.

"I've never told anyone any of that." As he absently began to rub his neck, he winced at the pain arcing through his arm. "You're right about me tensing up at old memories."

"Thank you for telling me. Now I understand why you always wanted to leave." She lifted their clasped hands to her lips and kissed the back of his hand. "Why did you never tell me this before?"

"I thought you might stop loving me."

"You didn't have a lot of faith in me, did you?" She stroked his cheek, softening her question.

Cole untangled their fingers. "You didn't even let me come to your house. I had to see you in secret. I was always worried you'd break up with me because I didn't wear the right clothes or have a car. What would it do to us to confess that I might have caused my family's deaths?"

"Was I really that awful? Why did you even bother with me?"

"Because I loved you." Cole took a deep breath to slow his pounding heart. "And I never thought you were awful. Just easily influenced."

"And now?"

Cole looked over at his son, sharing bread with the family from the special games as Dr. Allante admired the athlete's medal. The toddler ran among the pigeons, sending them flying. Even with two parents, they were a family on the cusp of chaos. How hard had it been for Bella?

"Now I think you're the strongest woman I know."

She nodded. "You're right. I was weak. I might have tried harder to contact you about being pregnant but I—I really didn't want to move away from my family."

"I hadn't realized the extent of Mrs. Beautemps's meddling when I saw that engagement announcement." Cole let loose a deprecating laugh. "I even imagined she might be trying to protect me—and she didn't even know me. I should have given you the chance to explain."

"Whether she intended to or not, she did protect you. You weren't in the right place to be saddled with a family. You would never have become the man you are today, and that would have been a loss for too many people who need you and your brilliance in the operating room." Her smile was sadly sweet. "As needy as I was, and with Adrian's complications, you could have never finished medical school while trying to provide for us, too. And I would have been in a strange environment without my family and friends, totally unprepared to be a wife and mother. Looking back, I see how her manipulations protected both of us."

"If I had asked you to marry me back then, would you have said yes?"

"I don't know." She bit her lip, reminiscent of that young, meek girl she had been. "I don't think so."

She gave him an open, gentle smile. "I always blamed you—for everything. It was as much me as you. Forgive me?"

A huge mass moved off Cole's heart. "I do. Forgive me, too?"

Her smile shone from her clear, bright eyes. "Yes, I do."

She lifted her face, her lips partially open. Cole gave in to instinct, leaned down…

And heard a woman's scream.

Bella looked up in time to see the toddler who had been feeding pigeons run from her mother straight into oncoming traffic. Faster than she could process, Bella saw the street corner saxophonist drop his sax and go after the girl.

In a split second of screaming, shouting and squealing brakes, he pushed the little girl to safety. The thud his body made hitting the front of the oncoming taxi was a sound Bella felt in the pit of her stomach.

Cole was already on his feet, running toward the scene.

"Bella, call 911."

Bella punched in the numbers and gave their location, all the while following in Cole's footsteps.

A quick look for Adrian showed him standing next to his grandfather, hands firmly gripping the wheelchair as if he was ready to push his grandfather from danger.

Cole knelt on the ground, trying to assess injuries, but the jazz player kept attempting to get up despite Cole's firm hand on his chest.

"How can I help?" She sounded much calmer than she felt.

Cole gave her an assessing look, then ordered, "Kneel down and bracket his head with your knees to hold him steady."

Isabella did as she was told, for once glad to have succinct commands to follow.

"The little girl—where's the little girl?" the man asked over and over, hysteria making his voice shrill.

Cole glanced up long enough to meet Bella's eyes. "Keep him talking and keep him calm."

Bella leaned in close to make eye contact with the injured man, firmly sandwiching his head between her knees.

Calmly, quietly, she answered, "The little girl is with her mother. You saved her. Now we are going to take care of you."

Cole emanated power and control. Lifting the man's shirt, he placed his hand on his stomach and gently pressed. "Does this hurt?"

The man bucked under Cole's light touch and started to shake. "Yes."

"Do you have any other pain?" Using the fingers of his free hand, Cole lifted one eyelid, then the other.

"My shoulder."

Cole continued with his assessment, running his hands down the man's legs, across his clavicle and down the other arm.

In the distance, she heard the siren of an ambulance. Controlling her adrenaline, she used her best sing-song hypnotherapist's tone as she smiled into the man's eyes. "What's your name?"

"Ernest." His voice was high and thready as his frantic focus darted everywhere at once. "Ernest Covington."

"Ernest." She said it forcefully to capture his attention. "That's a strong name. We're taking good care of you."

"The little girl?" he asked again, panic edging back into his voice as he started to gather his thoughts.

"She's okay. She's with her mother now." Bella didn't dare break eye contact to check the truth of that statement. Keeping Ernest's attention was key to keeping him calm. "Breathe with me, Ernest."

She stole a glance at Cole, who was counting off Ernest's pulse rate. Drawing from Cole's steadiness, Bella took in a steady breath, held it for a moment, then breathed it out again.

Ernest followed her lead. His own breath was jagged but he tried to follow her lead.

"Good. Let's do it again."

This time Ernest matched her tempo. The wildness in his eyes cleared. In a more measured tone, devoid of hysteria, he asked, "My saxophone. Where's my saxophone?"

"It's being well taken care of." At least, she hoped so.

Isabella sensed rather than saw Cole shift position. She wanted to read his assessment of Ernest but that was an indulgence she disciplined herself against.

With the greatest willpower she kept her attention centered on the injured man when she could have all too easily been drawn into Cole's charismatic presence.

In her peripheral vision Isabella saw the flashing lights of the ambulance. "Ernest, stay calm. The E.M.T.s are here to take you to the hospital."

The emergency medical technicians acted with speed and professionalism. Cole debriefed them with his assessment and Ernest was safely strapped to a backboard and loaded into the ambulance quicker than Bella thought possible.

Concussion, possible internal injuries, deep gash in the upper right arm, and a crushed shoulder was how Isabella interpreted Cole's medical jargon.

Without thinking, she leaned against Cole and allowed him to wrap her in his support as they watched the ambulance's lights fade into traffic.

Once she realized what she was doing, she almost shifted

away, too used to standing on her own feet, literally, to comfortably give up that modicum of control. But she'd slept in his arms the previous night. Moving away now seemed hypocritical.

And she sensed he needed her as much as she needed him. Or was that what she wanted to think?

"Will he make it?"

Cole looked grim. "I don't know."

Ernest had risked his life to save that little girl and now he might lose his own.

The father of the little girl gathered up the saxophone where it lay, scuffed from the pavement, and put it in the case that had filled with bills from compassionate onlookers.

The small affirmations of the goodness of human nature coupled with Ernest's heroic rescue and Cole's unhesitating response made tears well in Bella's eyes.

She wasn't the only one.

"Which hospital?" the father asked. "I want to..." he sniffed back tears before he could finish "...thank him and do what I can for him."

In unison, Cole and Bella both named their hospital.

"It's our local charity and teaching hospital," Bella explained. "They have excellent emergency medical staff and specialists there."

As he continued to thank Cole and Bella profusely, the father of the toddler gathered his family together, trying to calm his bewildered eldest son and his crying wife and babies. Finally, he herded them down the sidewalk toward the parking lot and their family car.

Isabella watched them until they turned a corner, out of sight.

She was grateful to see her own little family still safely at a distance. Adrian seemed to be entranced with his doctor doll while his grandfather steadily talked to him.

She felt the adrenaline that she had so tightly held in check now course through her, making her shake.

Cole held her tight. His strength kept her from falling apart right there on the street.

He whispered in her ear, "Deep breaths, Bella. You did a good job. He was already suffering from hypovolemic shock. He didn't need psychological shock compounding his condition. And you kept him alert despite his concussion. The trauma team will have a better chance of saving him in his present state of consciousness."

The strength in his deep tone more than his words steadied her.

She blinked and looked around, surprised to see everything looked the same. After such a dramatic incident she would have thought the earth would have cracked open, the Mississippi River would have started to flow backward or some other world-altering change would have taken place. A glance at her watch showed less than five minutes had passed. It seemed like a lifetime.

The backlash of all the excitement hit her. "How do the trauma teams do that every day? I'm exhausted."

"Training and natural aptitude."

"Give me a minute to settle down before Adrian sees me like this." The emotional roller coaster had left her feeling jumpy and snappish—not the best way to approach a child who might be traumatized. She forced herself to take a deep breath and let it out slowly, feeling her heart rate adjust accordingly.

"Okay, I'm ready." Despite the urgent need she felt to get to her child in case he needed comfort, she kept her walk to a fast clip instead of a full-out run.

Cole kept pace with her. "Are you always calm around Adrian? Has he ever seen you upset?"

As they began to walk, she saw Adrian pushing his grandfather toward them. He looked calm enough, but with Adrian looks were deceptive.

"Not if I can help it." She ignored the criticism she imagined in his voice—surely he knew he had no right?—and thought back. "I can't remember the last time Adrian might have seen me upset."

"Don't you think you're setting up unreasonable expectations? He's going to be exposed to the real world someday."

Isabella stopped walking and put her hands on her hips. "Just like that, you can come in and start parenting?"

Cole's jaw set as he stared into her eyes, his own eyes flashing. "I'd have been here sooner if I had known."

Maybe single parenthood hadn't been such a bad thing. She might have had to carry the whole load but she hadn't had to compromise on child-rearing techniques.

With a sharp glance at Adrian and her father, who were now within earshot, she said, "It's time for us to go home now."

"I'll walk you to your car."

"No need." Normalcy was what Isabella needed right now. And normalcy didn't include Cole Lassiter.

"I insist. It's the polite thing to do."

To refuse would be churlish and petty—which would upset her father. He would see her lack of manners as a sign of her distress and would become distressed himself on her behalf.

"Fine." Her tone was less than gracious.

Cole helped her father into the car, folded up and stored the wheelchair in her tiny trunk, and sternly instructed Adrian to buckle up in the backseat when her son protested against wearing his seat belt. All chores she dreaded. So why did she resent him taking that burden from her?

She was tired, too tired to be rational. The sooner she was home and in bed, the better. Although, with all that swirled in her mind, she could count on a case of insomnia to rob her of her much-needed rest.

She wouldn't think about how well she had slept in Cole's arms. She wouldn't think about never sleeping in his arms again. She wouldn't think about never sharing a bed again or growing old alone.

Cole interrupted her thoughts as he opened her car door for her.

Before she folded herself into her car, he put his hand on her arm to stop her. A shiver rushed through her at his touch—another thing she would never think of again.

"I'm going to be in town for the next several days. I want to spend time with my son."

"I'll call you tonight to discuss it after Adrian goes to bed."

"Isabella—"

The seriousness of his tone as well as the use of her given name put her on alert.

"Yes?"

"I wasn't asking you. I was telling you. Adrian is my son and I will spend time with him, with your blessing or without. You choose."

Isabella watched Cole stride away. He no longer had a cocky swagger of a boy trying to convince everyone, including himself, of his purpose. Now he walked with the confident step of a man sure of who he was and what he could do.

She squared her jaw. She was no longer the meek girl who agreed with everyone. She was a mother, and years of standing up for her son had made her stronger than Cole could ever imagine. If he thought he could bully her, he had another think coming.

CHAPTER NINE

COLE tried to work off his excess energy with a leisurely swim. Once he started, he didn't want to stop. The rhythmic motion not only helped to loosen up the stiff muscles in his shoulder and neck but also gave him the right environment to reflect.

He had come back to the home of his birth for a business venture, with the vague intention of proving to himself that he'd long ago recovered from his past—only to find he had created a future in his son.

And what did he have with his son's mother?

More than an attraction. A fascination, a longing, a connection that had never been severed despite his best attempts.

Over the past week he'd watched as she had selflessly, generously and cheerfully reached out to family and athletes alike at the special games. He'd never seen her lose her patience or her composure. Everyone who knew of her held her in the highest regard.

While he admired her saintly public persona, it was the private Bella that interested him. How many people knew she got grouchy when she was hungry? That she got riled when her parenting skills were questioned? That she purred when she slept?

And she screamed his name when she climaxed?

He was certain he was the only one with that knowledge.

And he wanted to know more.

But was he wasting his time? He had office staff scur-rying to rearrange schedules and other doctors shouldering his patient load.

When his muscles quivered and throbbed so hard that he could swim no more, he called it a night.

As a therapist, what would Bella say about his compul-sive swimming? Would she understand that he felt restless after so few hours in surgery the last week? Or would she see past that excuse and understand that he was afraid he'd stirred up too many ghosts today and was hoping to be so tired he would have a dream-free rest?

As a woman, what would she do to soothe him, body and soul?

He sat in his lonely hotel room, watching the shadows on the ceiling and remembering every curve, every moan, every delicious shudder Bella had gifted him with in this very room.

It was so much more than sex, but what it was, he just wasn't sure.

The R-word tried to creep into his mind but he stopped it before it could take hold. "Relationship" wasn't in his vo-cabulary. But, then, "Daddy" hadn't been there either, until his son had added it. Now it was one of the best words he'd ever heard.

Bella flipped through the photo albums her son loved so much as she thought about the last week and a half. With Cole on the scene, so much had changed—and so much would change in the future. The two of them standing slightly apart in a group photo gave her a sadly sweet feeling.

What did she feel for Cole? She had been angry at him for so long that anger kept resurfacing. But she had spoken the truth when she had assured him that going their own separate ways had been for the best for both of them. And now that she knew why he had wanted to leave so badly—why it hadn't been all about her—she had a whole different understanding of the life Cole had led apart from hers all those years ago.

She studied a photo taken at the boy-girl mixer where she had first met Cole. All her friends were posturing for the camera. She'd never noticed the boy in the background before. It was Cole, dressed in the white shirt and black pants of the wait staff, looking on with such longing to be a part of the class who kept him at arm's length. She was doing the same thing now—making sure he knew he was not part of her little family.

What did she feel for him?

The anger was a habit. A safety barrier to keep from getting hurt again. A way to punish Cole for all the pain she'd endured when he'd rejected her.

The lust…that was something more, something deeper she didn't want to explore, not with him leaving so soon.

But the relief she felt that she was no longer Adrian's sole parent was overwhelming.

And pride. After watching the competent, confident way Cole had tended to the saxophone player, she felt great pride in the man who had fought so hard to become the successful doctor he now was.

Isabella had intended to say no.

She had intended to tell Cole she had no intention of letting him waltz in fifteen years too late and take control. She had fought too long for her hard-won control to hand it over to him because he demanded it.

She had intended to tell him he could just put himself back on that airplane and never set foot again on New Orleans's soil. She didn't need to ever feel his arms around her again, or feel his breath as he whispered in her ear, or his mouth as he made her feel more like a woman than she had ever felt in her entire life.

She had intended to tell him that her son had been traumatized enough.

Except—Adrian hadn't been traumatized at all. Instead, he had been pretending to be a doctor, checking out all his superhero action figures like Cole had done, running his hands down their tiny arms and legs.

That Adrian initiated that kind of pretend game on his own was another huge breakthrough in his development.

How could she not be thrilled at Adrian's show of creativity?

And no matter how badly it stung her pride, Isabella would always do the right thing for her son.

She couldn't deny it. Cole was good for Adrian.

That Bella couldn't wrap her mind around the idea of never seeing Cole again was totally irrelevant in her decision-making process.

As always, she would do what was best for her son, even though getting used to Cole being around certainly wasn't good for her.

As she reached for the phone to give him a call, she noticed the message light.

Her department head requested—make that insisted—that she come in early to see a patient of Dr. Lassiter's. Did Cole understand what kind of havoc these last-minute schedule changes played with a single mother's schedule?

So he wanted to experience parenthood. Fine. If he wanted to experience parenthood, she'd let him, in all its glory.

As he mindlessly flipped through the television channels, Cole rubbed his shoulder, thought of the full prescription bottle on his bathroom counter and considered the talks he intended to have with his lawyers and his future partners in the morning. The medicine always made him thickheaded and groggy.

On the bedside table, his phone vibrated. Caller ID showed Bella's home number.

"Cole, I called to say okay."

"Okay?"

"Okay, you can spend time with Adrian while you're in town. Got a paper and pen? Here's his schedule."

Cole scrambled to keep up as Bella rattled off the whens and wheres of Adrian's day.

Adrian took the bus to the local junior high, where he was mainstreamed in morning classes for art, music, home economics and lunch. Bella picked him up and drove him across town for speech therapy during her lunch break. Then she drove him to track practice with his coach, an older woman who used to coach on a college level and now filled her days volunteering for the special games. Then Bella picked him up and took him back to her office where he had a space of his own to watch DVDs until she finished with all her clients.

"I'll take the lunch run and, instead of taking Adrian to your office, I'd just like to hang out with him, okay?"

Bella hesitated and he thought she was readying herself to say no.

Instead, she said, "If you have a problem, you can always bring him by the office or call David. Here's David's number."

Cole wrote it down under the list of Adrian's activities.

"Have him home by supper. We eat around seven."

"Will do." Cole's heart was pounding. After being without family for most of his life, he now had a son. "Thanks, Bella."

"Cole, one other thing."

Cole tensed at the unyielding tone of Bella's voice.

"What?"

"I'd rather not advertise that you're Adrian's father, especially around work."

Cole felt his heart plummet before his pride took hold.

"I may not have come from the best neighborhood, but few would hold me in contempt now."

"It's not about you. It's about me. Too many people know how to count and—I'm just not ready for the questions, asked and unasked, about my marriage to David. Give me some time."

Cole had sudden clarity of what it must have been like for Bella, unwed with her baby's father not returning her calls. Remorse struck him deeply. "I will be proud to announce to everyone that Adrian is my son, but we'll do this in your own time, Bella."

"In my own time. Thank you for that." Bella's sigh was deep and audible. "You're a father any child would be proud to have."

Fatherhood made Cole feel like a different man. His hope was that fatherhood would make him a better man. He vowed to Bella, to Adrian and to himself to do his best.

As Cole had a conference with his legal staff about Adrian's trust fund, he felt more than a sense of peace within himself. He felt a sense of legacy.

Legacy—an ideal he must have inherited from his father. Like his father, Cole wouldn't be handing his legacy to his son. Adrian had limitations—even though Cole had a strong feeling his son was far from reaching the end of his abilities yet.

Unlike his father, Cole was more than content with who his son was. Having a son was a gift Cole had never even hoped for. That his son had autism was a reality Cole would need to learn more about.

But Cole didn't need a clone of himself to make him proud of being a parent. And professionally he had successfully spread his own legacy throughout the United States with the sports medicine and orthopedic clinics he supported. He found plenty of fulfilment in handing his knowledge to surgeons across the nation. With the New Orleans connection, he would have all the major areas covered.

For the first time since he'd stepped off the plane at the New Orleans airport—no, for the first time since he'd boarded an airplane at the same airport fifteen years ago—Cole felt at peace.

Today he finally felt like he should move on, past the death of his parents and brother and into his own future. The past was the past. If he had to name the cause of his recovery, that name would be Isabella.

Bella had given him so much. A son. Absolution for so many past transgressions. A sense of belonging—at least, he was working on that one. Bella was right. He couldn't expect her to disrupt her life and their son's life for him.

Now to set up a meeting with the sports clinic and convince the doctors they needed him to relocate to New Orleans.

Glad to put all the legal dealings behind him, Cole went in search of his patients. While the details of business were important, they never satisfied him like medicine did.

He found Heath Braden, the young fireman, in the rehab lab, slowly walking on the treadmill. The bleakness had left his eyes, a vast improvement from the last time Cole had seen him.

"Thanks for sending Ms. Allante, Doc." Heath held out his left hand for a cordial shake. "At first, I wasn't sure about all that mind-over-matter stuff, but we did this biofeedback thing with wires stuck on my head to measure my brainwaves to know when I'm getting my thoughts in the right place. It seems to be working."

"So you're not in as much pain?"

"Yeah, I am. But then I just remember the way I was thinking when we did the biofeedback thing and try to re-create that same place in my mind." Heath held up his braced hand.

"It's not that the pain goes away, but more like it's not the main thing going on with me. It's like hearing annoying noise in the background instead of blasting through headphones. Ms. Allante is fantastic."

"I totally agree with you there." Last night, once he had finally got to sleep, he had dreamed of her all night long. He'd woken up before his alarm had gone off, feeling happy and excited to meet the coming day. "Have you seen Dr. Wong today?"

"Sure. He sat in with me and Ms. Allante. He said he'd never seen her work before and wanted to check her out."

Cole remembered the way Wong had checked her out at the dance. "And what did he think?"

"He said he would like to refer more patients to her."

"I understand she stays booked."

"That's what she told him. That I was a special case she worked in because you had asked her to." Heath chuckled. "Dr. Wong wanted to know what you had that he didn't. Ms. Allante got all flustered. I don't think she even realized he was flirting with her until then."

Cole checked his watch. Did he have time to speak to Dr. Wong before he needed to pick up Adrian? If he did, what would he say?

He had no claim on Bella and he never would. Bella deserved a man who could give her emotional support. All Cole had to give was a boatload of emotional baggage.

"I'll be here a few more days, Heath. If you need anything, let me know."

"Dr. Wong tells me you invented the techniques he used to keep from amputating."

"That's what sharing knowledge is all about." Cole had such a good feeling about this merger, despite some of the sports clinic doctors' reluctance to agree to as much charity work as Cole required in his merger agreements. But they would come around. They needed his expertise.

Heath held up his healing hand. His voice was gruff with tears as he said, "Without this, I don't know who I'd be. Thanks, Doc, for everything."

Thanks like Heath's was why Cole did what he did. He might not be gifted in love, but he'd been gifted with a double dose of talent in hand surgery. Nothing made him feel more fulfilled than to spread as much good as he could.

"You're welcome. Take care of that family of yours."

"Thanks to you, Doc, I will."

Cole's next stop was to check on Ernest. According to the charts, Ernest's anxiety over being in the hospital was playing havoc with his vitals.

"Tell me the truth, Doc." Ernest gestured toward his braced shoulder. "How bad is it?"

From what Cole had seen of the X-rays, Ernest's complete recovery was possible if he had the right specialist.

"You'll need surgery. The sooner the better. And physical therapy."

"I can't afford all that." Ernest took a deep, soulful breath. "Music is my bliss, Doc. But without my shoulder working, I can't make music. And without my bliss, I have no life."

Cole flexed his own hand. "Let me see what I can do."

The sports clinic had picked up the tab for Heath. Lassiter Hand and Wrist Institute would do the same for Ernest if Dr. Lockhart would perform the operation. Two charity cases. Two opportunities to give back. It was a good way to begin a partnership.

The alarm on Cole's watch beeped, reminding him that he needed to pick up Adrian in fifteen minutes. Where had the morning gone?

His admiration for Bella was growing by leaps and bounds,

as was his determination that he would make life easier for her from here on out.

How could he do that from New York?

The merger was based on certain people being in certain places. How hard would it be to relocate to New Orleans?

How often would he be in town even if he moved?

And, in the end, would Bella even want him around all the time? She had made it very clear that she based all her decisions on him being a temporary part of her life. At this point she had good reason to.

He swung by the cafeteria, picked up the supersize subway sandwich and two apples he hoped to share and went in search of Bella.

He found her in the physical therapy department, jotting down notes between patients.

"Cole—Dr. Lassiter," she corrected herself. "I saw your fireman this morning, the one your office called my office about."

She sounded professional and distant, as if they hadn't shared the weekend of a lifetime together. While Cole understood the division between home and hospital—he had dated plenty of medical professionals—he hadn't been prepared for the formal attitude from Bella.

"I know."

"As you know, I was out of the office most of last week and my policy is that I don't take business calls when I'm out as I reserve my free time for my son. So I didn't get the message personally delivered by the hospital director until I checked my business voicemail last night. That's quite some weight you pull, Dr. Lassiter."

Usually Cole would take that as a compliment, but from Bella's tone Cole knew that was not what Bella had intended.

"Thank you, Isabella, for taking on Heath as a patient."

"All it took was rescheduling existing patients, making

arrangements with David to get Adrian onto his bus on time this morning and coming in two hours early. Who needs sleep anyway?" The dark circles under Bella's eyes underscored her legitimate complaint.

Cole understood so much more about Bella than he had when he'd made that call. In this case he'd earned the cliché of arrogant doctor. He'd justified his high-handedness as being what was best for the patients but had never given a thought about the personal lives of those he ordered around. Bella was showing him a bigger world.

"Point taken."

"Perhaps next time you could use some of your formidable influence to have the hospital staff add an additional CBT. But, then, after this week there won't be a next time, will there?"

He wanted to say, yes, he was here to stay. But the partnership merger wasn't formalized yet. And he was about to make the details shaky—especially those pertaining to him and his base location—and he had no right to reveal confidences.

Secrets. He was really beginning to hate them.

After Cole left, Isabella munched on the apple Cole had left her, making herself eat even when her nervous stomach protested. She had to keep her health up to be a good mother.

Gloria, a physical therapist Isabella often worked with, walked into the break room, puzzlement in her eyes. "Was that Dr. Lassiter?"

"Yes." How much had Gloria overheard?

Isabella hated the sharp tone she had used with Cole. She hadn't meant to. Only all her fears had come to the surface as she'd realized she was trusting this man with her son.

And she wanted to trust him with her heart.

Gloria shuffled through the plastic containers in the refrigerator, coming up with her own bowl of salad. "You were really putting him in his place, weren't you? You go, girl!"

Apparently, Gloria had heard enough.

"I guess I did." Isabella gave her a sheepish smile as she unwrapped the sandwich Cole had brought her—the sandwich she hadn't even thanked him for. She never did that, never had a lapse of manners. But, then, she'd never before let loose on a doctor like she'd just let loose on Cole. What was Cole doing to her?

She gave Gloria a wink. "I hope I didn't bruise his ego."

"Don't worry. There are plenty of women on staff who'll be more than glad to kiss him and make him feel better." Gloria shook the almost empty bottle of salad dressing, trying to squeeze out the last little bit.

Isabella couldn't keep herself from asking, "Which ones?"

That stopped Gloria in midmotion. "You're interested in him, aren't you?"

She wanted to deny it, but now that she had acknowledged him, at least to her family, as Adrian's father, denial felt too much like hypocrisy. Besides, her blush gave her away without a word. "We've got past history together."

Saying it aloud felt so freeing.

"Oh?" Obviously, Gloria wanted to hear more but Isabella took an extra-large bite of her sandwich to keep from talking.

And Gloria was intuitive enough to change the subject. "You're sticking around for lunch today? Is Adrian okay?"

Gloria always took a passing interest in Adrian. Many times Isabella sensed that she and Gloria could become good friends—if only she had the time.

"I've made other arrangements." She was so used to being independent. But she could really use a reassuring platitude or two right now. "I'm letting someone else take Adrian to speech therapy today and I'm worried about how he'll react to the change in his routine."

"Probably like we all react to change. We're uncomfortable at first then we decide it's not nearly as bad as we thought it would be." Gloria gave her a sympathetic smile. "My daughter had her first sleepover at a friend's house the other night. I have to confess, I cried after I dropped her off, then cruised around the block for at least fifteen minutes in case she called, wanting me to pick her up and bring her home."

"At least you didn't hide in the bushes and peek in the windows. That's what I would have done."

Gloria gave her a grin. "Who says I didn't?"

"Thanks. It helps to know I'm not alone in this overprotective motherhood thing."

Gloria nodded. "My husband had a hard time sympathizing with me. I think that's where men balance us out. While it might bother them just as much to let our children spread their wings, they see it as inevitable and just do it."

"With Adrian's autism, I worry more."

"Maybe it just feels that way. All our kids are special in their own ways. We all worry." Impulsively, Gloria have her a little hug. "I've gotta run, but call me sometime. We'll get together and commiserate—or laugh at ourselves, whichever fits at that moment."

"I will. Thanks." Yes, Isabella needed to make time for friends. She needed to make a life for herself.

She had Cole to thank for giving her the opportunity to realize that about herself.

As Isabella munched the half sandwich Cole had brought her, she wished she could have that conversation all over again.

Her nerves were frayed, and Cole was the cause, but that was no reason to take out her frustrations on him.

She grinned to herself, thinking of how well he had satisfied her frustrations in bed—which made her wish they could have another night together—which made her frustrated all over again.

Thankfully, she had her work to lose herself in, although she had to take extra care to keep her unsettled attitude out of the patients' sessions.

A few days. She could be flexible for a few days while Cole and Adrian bonded.

In fact, if she tried really hard, she might even enjoy herself.

Before she changed her mind, she made a phone call to the manicurist on the corner to schedule the basics. She wasn't sure what she would trim from the budget, but she would make the money stretch.

Would Cole come through with the financial support he had promised? Yes, she was sure he would. She had no reason to trust him, but she did. Then again, throwing money at a problem when there was plenty to throw was fairly easy and required little commitment—or so she remembered from days gone by.

"Hello, Suzette? I would like to make an appointment, please. Let's go with a manicure, okay?"

A sense of well-being flooded through her. For once she was following her own advice and taking care of herself.

And she knew, deep down, she didn't need to worry about Adrian while she was being pampered. Cole would take good care of their son.

Sure, she left Adrian in David's care, but she always felt beholden, knowing David was doing her a favor despite his protests that he didn't mind at all.

Truthfully, while David couldn't be a better friend, he had never felt like Adrian's surrogate father.

Leaving Adrian in Cole's care felt different—like he was doing his share instead of a favor. She felt no guilt, only the slightest apprehension. Cole might not handle parenting the way she would, but Adrian would be safe and nurtured.

She redialed the number for Suzette. "This is Isabella Allante again. Could we add a pedicure, too, with a hand and foot massage?"

Smiling with satisfaction, Isabella hung up the phone.

Thanks to Cole, her bad mood was now completely gone.

CHAPTER TEN

ON THE drive home, Isabella couldn't stop looking at her fresh pearl-pink nail polish. She felt guilty yet exhilarated for the hour she had stolen from her busy day to be pampered. When had the last time been she had done something solely to delight herself instead of for someone else? She couldn't remember. Having her nails done made her feel like her own person again, instead of a mother, or a therapist, or a volunteer.

Through the open windows of her home Isabella inhaled the scent of shrimp and butter and garlic balanced by the tangy odor of tomatoes and okra with a sweet sidenote of banana pudding. She breathed in, savoring the aroma.

But why was it so quiet? Her house was never quiet at this time of day. Adrian always had televisions blaring in at least three different rooms.

But she heard no noise from those open windows, no blasting of a video on the television, just a calm that she had never associated with her home before.

A thousand scenarios rolled through her mind, all of them involving ambulances. She swung open the door, expecting to see vestiges of chaos.

Instead, sitting on the couch, side by side, were the two main men in her life, Cole and Adrian. Cole was reading aloud from the book in his lap while Adrian held his own book and a new oversize stuffed animal, a snarling wolf.

Cole glanced up over his glasses—since when had he worn glasses?—and winked. "Almost done here. There's a bottle of wine chilling in the kitchen. Pour us both a glass, okay? And there's grape juice in the fridge for Adrian."

Stunned, Isabella did as she was told, bringing the drinks in on a tray.

Cole raised his glass to her. "Truce?"

She clinked glass on glass. "Truce."

By the time they had drunk to their armistice, Adrian was rocking and flapping, upset with the interruption of his story.

"Please, continue," she told Cole, before Adrian went into meltdown mode.

She settled into her favorite chair and watched in amazement as Cole read the manga version of *Call of the Wild* to her son, who sat still enough to listen.

Adrian had his own copy of the book. He studied the pictures, flipping pages when Cole did. Every time Cole said the word "wolf", Adrian would pat the toy wolf tucked under his arm.

As Cole finished up the last few pages of the book, Isabella leaned back in her chair and closed her eyes, letting the baritone of his voice roll through her.

Would this be her life if she and Cole were married? Evenings of contentment followed by nights of…

She took a sip of wine as she allowed her imagination to flow. Nights of lovemaking so wild she and Cole would end up totally relaxed, totally spent and thoroughly connected so far beyond the physical they could read each other's thoughts and feelings.

She wanted that dream so badly it made her ache inside to know it could never be. Cole would be going back to New York by the end of the week. She'd heard it all over the hospital today even though he hadn't told her yet.

"'The End.'" He closed the book with a snap. "Now let's eat."

"That was…" Words failed Bella.

"That was our third time through tonight. I think we've outgrown *Thomas the Train*." Cole smiled, quite pleased with himself, then stood and headed toward the kitchen.

Isabella had never gotten Adrian to sit still long enough for even one reading of *Thomas the Train*, and now her baby was listening to Jack London.

She felt…inadequate. It wasn't a pretty feeling.

Books for Adrian were few and far between in her house, except for picture books specially designed to aid his communication skills. She hadn't upgraded Adrian's reading material since those early toddler books because she'd seen no need. He had no interest in books—at least, he never had before now—and he'd never sat still enough to listen, no matter how hard she'd tried.

When had been the last time she'd tried? Between her work and Adrian's school and therapy sessions and her father's care at the nursing home, she barely had time to keep their clothes clean and their bellies full. The phrase "bad mother" came to mind.

In her small kitchen with her small dining table, she dodged and swerved, trying to avoid brushing against Cole. Still, whether they touched or not, she felt too much awareness, too much remembrance of being touched, stroked, loved.

No, not loved. Cole had given her no indication that he loved her. Forgiveness was not love. But it was a start.

Isabella sighed as she grabbed a handful of silverware from the drawer. There was no starting with Cole. Only ending. And the sooner they ended this unidentifiable thing between them, the better. Cole was here to get acquainted with his son. That was all he'd asked for. That was all she'd allowed for.

Robotically, Isabella set out plates, forks and knives while Adrian stuffed napkins into napkin rings, her monogrammed linen and sterling reminders of days gone by. From the corner of her eye she watched as he processed three place settings instead of two.

He moved the napkin and ring at his plate to Cole's and then back to his before going to the linen drawer and retrieving another napkin ring and napkin.

With a triumphant grin he looked at her for approval. Normally, she would have made a big deal of this new breakthrough in flexibility, but today she just gave him a discreet nod, sensing Adrian wouldn't want his father to think he didn't always make these kinds of adjustments.

Yes, she hated to admit it, but Cole had been right. She had fallen into a rut with Adrian, not stretching his boundaries or pushing his comfort zone.

What would happen when Cole went away? She knew she wouldn't be able to fill in the holes he would leave. Would Adrian regress? Would she?

Bella took another sip of wine. She would survive like she always did, one day at a time—one second at a time if need be.

And she would do what she could for her son.

Somehow, tonight, she didn't feel as responsible for Adrian's emotional state as usual. That felt both selfish and exhilarating—and right. A mother shouldn't always identify with her son's emotions, even if that son had emotional as well as developmental issues.

Bella stood on tiptoe to grab a serving dish from a top shelf. Cole reached over her, his body pressed against hers, to snag the plate for her.

As he handed it to her, their hands touched and she pulled back, dropping the dish.

She flinched as it hit the floor, but it stayed intact. Cole gallantly scooped it up, this time holding on to it himself, and dished up the gumbo from the pot on the stove.

Once he put it on the table, he turned to her.

"Something wrong?" Cole rubbed his neck, looking askance.

She realized she'd been staring at him. "No. Everything's fine. More than fine. Everything looks wonderful." She was babbling. Taking a breath, she asked, "Does your neck ache?"

"A bit." The way his eyes darted away from hers, she could tell he hurt more than just a bit. Ironic how father and son communicated in the same way, even though they'd never met until now.

She should have tried harder—or at least kept trying through the years. But looking back did none of them any good.

Cole held her chair as she took her seat, a nicety that made her feel even more awkward in her own kitchen.

As she picked up her spoon to eat, she said, "I took advantage of you being with Adrian and I stopped on my way home and got my nails done."

"I noticed."

"Really?"

"I'm a hand doctor. I notice hands." He picked up his own spoon. "Yours fascinate me."

"Why?"

He leaned in close, his voice deep and his eyes black and intense. "Because I know what they can do."

"Don't." She pulled back, taking a deep sip of wine. "We're not a couple. We can't be a couple. You'll be leaving soon and—"

"And?" He studied her until she squirmed. "What if I weren't leaving?"

"And what if pigs flew?" She dragged her spoon through her gumbo. "I thought we called a truce."

"But we weren't fighting."

"We soon will be if I get any hungrier." She forced her tone to sound like playful banter then dropped the pretense. "I'm on too much of an emotional roller coaster to play games with you, Cole. And we've got Adrian to consider."

He nodded. "No games."

Picking up their tension, Adrian began drumming his spoon and fork on the table.

Cole looked up over his glasses. "Your mother says 'no games', son. Eat."

Miraculously, her son did as he was told.

With no better option Isabella did the same, determined to concentrate on the present and deal with the future when she had to. Survival.

Her first bite of the gumbo was heaven. "Where did you learn to cook?"

She hadn't meant to encourage conversation, but the question was innocuous enough, wasn't it?

He shrugged modestly then frowned, as if a painful thought had crossed his mind. "I've cooked since I could reach the stove. During school, when my brother and I couldn't go out on the boat with our parents, we were in charge of supper."

That commonality called out to her so strongly, she couldn't help but respond. "I still miss my mother. With the long hours my father worked, mealtimes were often the only times we were together. Then, afterward, Mrs. Beautemps kept me so involved in outside activities, I hardly ever ate at home."

Cole did that to her—made her respond even when she didn't want to. He always had. She had once found it freeing to let go of her control when she was with him, saying what she wanted to say, feeling what she wanted to feel.

"I wonder if my father felt lonely after that, eating by himself all those nights?"

"As a man who takes most of his meals alone, I can tell you that it gets old."

She looked at him, really looked at him—at the gray at his temples, the set of his shoulders, the shadows in his eyes.

Cole wiped his mouth under her scrutiny—which brought attention to the lips Bella longed to taste.

"I'm sorry. Sad memories aren't appropriate dinner topics, are they?" he said.

She touched Adrian's juice glass to encourage him to drink, an automatic reflex she should have dropped long ago as he had outgrown his picky appetite for several years now.

"I'm not used to making polite conversation at my table. I guess I save it for the fundraising parties."

Cole lifted his glass in salute. "I'm in the same boat with you."

The rest of the meal was small talk about Cole and Adrian's swim in the hospital pool and their trip to the bookstore and about hospital gossip.

There were silent moments with nothing but the scrape of forks and shuffle of napkins that bordered between awkward and pleasant. With a little more practice they would soon feel like a real family.

She had to stop this. Now.

She looked at her son, so content to have his father at the table with him.

Had the damage already been done?

How long would it take to become used to not having Cole around again? How bad would the trauma be in the interim?

Bella admitted to herself she wasn't only worried for Adrian's sake.

The shrimp and rice dish suddenly became very heavy in her stomach as Isabella realized it was too late. When Cole left, he would take a piece of her with him—just like last time.

She covered her mouth with her napkin, not sure she could control herself enough to hide her feelings.

No, not again. But she couldn't deny it.

She was in love with Cole. And this time it was a love so much deeper, so much bigger, so much more invasive.

I will spend time with my son, Cole had said. It was his right.

She couldn't stop him any more than she could stop herself from loving him.

What choice did she have but to see this through?

As she had always done to survive, she focused on the basics of her existence. Live for the moment. Live for Adrian. Love Cole.

She had no other choices.

Somewhere between napkin up and napkin down, Bella changed. Cole wasn't sure what it was, but it was definitely a change.

Next to him, Adrian thumped his fork, impatient for the next part of the plan they had devised together that afternoon.

Interpreting Bella's mercurial mood would have to wait. They would have time later to talk once Bella agreed to the plan.

"Dessert?" He scraped his chair back, opened a couple of cabinets until he found the dessert bowls, and scooped up helpings of rich banana pudding for each of them.

"I'm so full…" Bella protested.

"Just taste it." Cole smiled at her. "I made it just for you, remembering this was your favorite dessert."

"You remembered that after all these years?"

He had remembered so much, no matter how hard he had

tried to forget. But he would file that bittersweet thought under inappropriate dining topics.

"You have to taste it. It's part of the plan."

"The plan?" The wary look in her eyes was not a good sign.

He gestured with his spoon. "The pudding."

"Momma," Adrian encouraged her.

She took a long look at her son before nodding.

"All right." Taking a bite, Bella made an ecstatic face very reminiscent of a certain night together. "Mmm. So good."

"Thank you. It was nothing. Just a little thing I threw together."

"False modesty doesn't fit you."

You fit me. Cole had sense enough not to say it, although he couldn't swear he didn't show it in every muscle of his body.

He waited until Bella finished her serving, pleased to note she had found room, even though she had declared herself full.

"I have a favor to ask."

She rested her hand on her stomach. "You're taking unfair advantage."

He noted the warning beneath her lighthearted tone—but he would do anything for his son.

"Yes. Fingers crossed that it works." He tried to look charming, using the smile that had earned him many women's favors in the past. "There's a big convention coming and the hotel is booked. I need a place to stay for the next few days. You've got a spare bedroom. I was hoping—"

"No." Bella's response was immediate, explosive, threatened.

Cole sat back and let the fear fade from her eyes.

Fear. "What are you afraid of, Bella?"

She cast a sideways look at Adrian. "Not in front of the c-h-i-l-d."

"Adrian isn't a child anymore."

"There—that's one reason. You undermine my parenting."

"I don't…" Maybe he did.

Sensing his weakness, Bella took full advantage. "You've never been a parent before."

"Maybe not. But you've never been a fourteen-year-old boy before. I have."

He dared her to say that Adrian was different. In some ways, yes, Adrian wasn't a typical teenager. But in so many other ways he was a normal adolescent boy going through the roller-coaster ride of puberty, trying to fit into a world where he knew deep down he would always be on the outside looking in.

Yes, Cole understood a lot of what lurked beneath the surface of Adrian's exterior.

"Daddy." Adrian flapped his hand and rocked so fast he was on the verge of oversetting his chair. "Stay."

"Oh, honey. Daddy can't. He's got to go back to New York."

"Adrian and I already talked about that."

"Well, you apparently didn't make it very clear, did you?"

Adrian pushed his chair back and took off running for the stairs.

"See what you've done." Bella's face flushed and her eyes sparked as she thrust her finger at him.

She was beautiful in all her protective maternal glory, a woman he was proud to call the mother of his child. What would she do if he leaned over and covered her mouth with his own? Would she taste of fire and passion as she had yesterday?

He had to pull his mind back to their discussion. He had to win this one for his son.

"What have I done? Upset your safe, boring little world?" He pointed up the stairs. "You yourself said Adrian has advanced being around me—even if you said it grudgingly."

The sound of Adrian clomping down the stairs had them both drawing back into silent glares and crossed arms.

Adrian plopped his calendar down in front of them. Blue checks marked the remaining days of the week. He mashed his thumb onto each check mark. "Stay. Stay. Stay. Stay. Stay."

Then he sadly stroked a poorly drawn airplane on the last day of the week before waving goodbye.

Bella looked stunned.

Cole tried to keep his smugness from showing, but he didn't try very hard. "So what's it going to be, Bella? Can I stay? For my son?"

Bella looked from the face of her hopeful son to the face of her hopeful son's father. She closed her eyes as if to shut out both father and son then took a deep breath.

That was when Cole knew what her answer would be.

"Yes. You can stay until you leave for New York." She turned to Adrian, putting her finger on the airplane drawing. "But he has to go to his house on Saturday."

Cole held up a hand and Adrian slapped it. High five. Something else he'd taught his touch-averse son today. A surprise he'd been saving for Bella.

But maybe she'd had enough surprises for one day. She just stared at the air where their hands had met before saying, "I'm going for a walk. You two, do the dishes while I'm gone."

When Adrian frowned his reluctance, she shrugged it off. "Consider it part of your father's room and board."

Cole recognized Bella's domestic chore assignment for what it was, an attempt to reclaim control. By the loud bang of the front door, she might need to make that walk extra-long.

* * *

Bella lay in bed, knowing Cole was only a bedroom wall away.

Was he thinking about their night—and morning—together, as she was? She held her breath, the better to hear any noise in the next room. Was that tossing and turning she was hearing?

When David had learned of her temporary guest, he hadn't said anything, but he hadn't had to. His tight-lipped nod had said it all.

They so rarely argued. She tried to think of an olive branch to extend in apology, but she wasn't sorry. Not sorry about Cole staying over anyway. Maybe a little sorry that she'd thrown into David's face that he often had guests in his home.

She had always been a little jealous, not because they had once been married but that she was alone and he wasn't.

He should be happy for her—and Cole wasn't even staying over in "that" way. But she also understood. David didn't want to see her hurt, didn't want to have to pick up the pieces when she fell apart, like she had done a decade and a half ago.

But he would. He would put his arm around her shoulder, let her cry until there were only gasping sobs, then wipe her tears and hold her until she no longer felt like she was unraveling at the seams.

David was right. Letting Cole stay was a mistake—a big one.

Every inch of her, every cell of her, cried out for Cole.

Only grasping her pillow tight kept her from leaving her bed to seek out Cole's. She had a young, impressionable son in the house. And Cole would be gone within the week. Two good reasons to keep her distance, even though her imagination supplied her with the texture of Cole's skin, the deep growl in his throat as she turned him on, the mingled scent of their bodies after they'd made love.

Knowing only a thin wall stood between them was torture.

On her nightstand the clock ticked one second at a time, mocking her.

It was going to be a long night.

CHAPTER ELEVEN

AWKWARD didn't begin to describe the way Bella felt the next morning. What if she met Cole in hallway?

She had never wished for a spaghetti-strapped wisp of nothingness with a matching silk wrapper before, but she did so now.

Dressed in her voluminous, faded, flannel granny gown, she did what she could with the lip gloss she found in her sock drawer, before heading for the bathroom.

The hallway was clear. Only two more steps—

Cole opened the door to the bathroom at the same time she reached for the door handle.

And there he was, in nothing but his gym shorts, the same gym shorts he'd worn when she had dropped her towel for him in his hotel room.

As she stared, he rubbed his hand across his chest hair. Bella remembered in detail how that coarse texture felt under her own palm.

She wanted to reach out and feel Cole's warmth, wanted to feel his hand glide over her bare shoulder, wanted—wanted with a desire stronger than she had ever felt before.

"Good morning, Bella." Cole's sleep-husky voice sent shivers through her.

She felt her nipples peak and chanced a glance down, now grateful for the thick coverage of her dowdy gown.

Before she could discipline herself, her glance drifted further. She couldn't help but smile.

"Good morning to you, too." Her own voice was raspy, breathy—everything a *femme fatale* could wish for.

The squeak of their fourteen-year-old son's door opening had them both jumping back and looking anywhere but at each other.

"I'll make sure Adrian gets on the bus this morning." Cole eased out around her, brushing his hand across her sleeve and jerking back like he'd been burned. An accident? She hoped not.

"Thanks." Bella barely withstood the temptation to let her shoulder rub against his chest as she passed him. "I'll see you tonight."

Once inside the bathroom, she was grateful to find the mirror so steamed up she could avoid confronting her flushed face.

Tonight. It would be so easy to slip into Cole's room, into Cole's bed, with none the wiser but the two of them. They had already done it once—make that three times.

But Bella couldn't deny that this time would be different. This time would mean commitment, at least for her.

Bella's breath caught as she realized she had already given her heart to Cole—or maybe she'd never taken it back all those years ago. If she gave him her body, too, how could she ever let him walk away again?

She needed time. Time to think. Time to decide to let go or pull back. Time to gather her defenses if he didn't feel the same—and she had no indication he did, did she?

At the hospital, Isabella jumped every time she heard the intercom crackle until she learned that Cole would be tied up all morning with an internet video consultation. Most surgeons said that the mental aspects of the video consultant were much more brutal than performing the actual surgery.

She realized Cole was doing everything he could to stay in New Orleans and get to know his son without jeopardizing his patients' care. His dedication only made her love him more.

And that love made her dread going home to him. Isabella had already lived through unrequited love. Why did she have to fall in love again—with the very man who hadn't loved her enough the first time?

So that night Isabella surprised Gloria and several other colleagues by joining them at the local coffee bar after work.

Not ready to live too dangerously, she ordered the decaffeinated version of her favorite coffee-based indulgence but did have real whipped cream on top. After forty-five minutes of stress-relieving laughs, she found her determination to keep the relationship with Cole casual and light, at least on the outside.

Distractedly, Cole read to Adrian while listening for Bella's car. The aroma of cooling pizza drifted from the kitchen.

She had called and left a message that she would be a few minutes late while he was in consultation. Cole had never called to report his comings and going to anyone. What would it be like to have someone care if you were coming home or not and then worry if you were late?

For the fifth time that evening he read the manga version of *Call of the Wild*. "Wolf, wolf, wolf, wolf, wolf," he said in fast succession while Adrian patted his stuffed wolf as fast as he could. It was a game Cole had invented to break the monotony of reading the same book over and over. Tomorrow merited another trip to the bookstore.

Cole made a mental note to tell Bella he would be in surgery in the afternoon and wouldn't be able to take Adrian where he needed to go. He didn't take lightly that he had asked—demanded—to spend time with his son and now would have to make other arrangements.

How had Bella managed Adrian's complex schedule all these years? David had helped. But Adrian wasn't David's responsibility. Were there carers trained in looking after children with autism who could be called on to take the stress off parents?

When Bella burst into the door, Cole noticed the strain at the corner of her eyes had lessened the smallest bit. He vowed he would do what he could to ease her burdens. Relocating to New Orleans would help.

"Smells great." Bella took a deep breath to emphasize her appreciation of the pizza.

Living in the same house with Bella and Adrian would help even more. Cole put that thought behind him. "I hope you still like sausage and mushroom."

"Yes, I do. At least, I think I do. I usually get plain cheese pizza for Adrian."

The sacrifices she had made for his son knew no bounds. Bella had already entered into one loveless marriage for her son—a marriage that had left scars when it had fallen apart. He could still hear the hurt in her voice when she talked of her ex-mother-in-law turning her back on her and Adrian. He would never ask her to marry without love again.

"We have a cheese pizza for Adrian and a pepperoni one for me." She gave him a brilliant smile as he pulled out her chair. Bella appreciated the niceties more than any woman he had ever met. He loved to indulge her, as her femininity called forth the gentleman in him.

He would teach Adrian to pull out his mother's chair. The gesture would give Adrian a sense of pride, like it did for him.

Yes, the decision to move to New Orleans was the right one. If only the partners at the sports center would agree, his lawyers were standing by, waiting to amend the merger agreement.

Bella lifted the lids on each of the pizza boxes. "A pizza apiece? We're quite a diverse family, aren't we?"

Family. She'd said it so easily. Did she even realize she'd included him?

Adrian waved his arms over his head and back down again while kicking his feet. "Daddy," he said.

No awkward pauses tonight.

"Adrian is learning the butterfly stroke at the pool." Cole helped himself to a serving of pizza.

"Daddy is teaching you?"

"It's a difficult stroke but Adrian has it all figured out." No man could be prouder of his son than Cole was of Adrian.

Sharing parenting responsibility would be easier if they lived close to each other.

Maybe he could find a house nearby? Or a duplex like the one Bella had shared with David? Would she prefer the neighborhood she'd grown up in or would she rather stay in this one?

Neither of them were the kind of people to live with someone else on a permanent basis without commitment. Those arrangements always ended acrimoniously and Cole could never let Adrian be caught in the middle.

Adrian held up his hand and Cole high-fived it, like they had been practicing. According to his teachers, Adrian had been making phenomenal progress. Cole's heart swelled to hear he was part of it. Did Bella think he had been a good influence on his son? It was so hard to know what Bella thought. She hid herself so well. Would she ever trust him enough to let him see past that disciplined facade?

If only Bella loved him…

CHAPTER TWELVE

LAST night Bella had been stunned when Cole and Adrian had slapped hands. But tonight she was shocked. Delighted. Pleased. Jealous. And overwhelmed.

All because of Cole. He was so good for Adrian.

If only he was good for her, too. But that was a selfish thought, unworthy of a mother. Isabella focused on her son's accomplishment and pushed her own needs out of her mind.

She'd heard and read of massive breakthroughs like Adrian was experiencing, but she'd never expected it to happen for her son.

Tonight Adrian had initiated the action and used it as a sign to communicate.

She had been trying to get him to use signs, symbols—anything to indicate yes or no—since he was born. Cole had come into their lives and within days had her son communicating beyond what years of therapy and home training had accomplished.

At Cole's nod, Adrian left the table, put on oven mitts to reach into the oven and came back carrying a blackberry cobbler.

His glance skittered across her face, then across Cole's.

Under control again, she grinned at both of them. "Another bribe? What's this one for?"

While Cole dished up a helping of cobbler with a side of

ice cream for her, Adrian rummaged in his backpack and produced a sheet of crumpled, slightly watermarked paper and shoved it next to her along with a pen.

Adrian touched her dessert bowl, urging her to take a bite as she had done so often for him in the past.

Automatically, she did.

"Very good," she complimented sincerely.

"Adrian was hoping to enter the local special games swimming competition this coming Saturday."

She really didn't have the time to add another sport to her son's busy schedule—not after Cole left them.

"Momma," Adrian added, giving her that bright smile of his.

How could she say no to that?

"Two against one. Unfair odds, I'd say." She looked from one to the other, so alike in so many ways. The swim meet was on Saturday. She could cut her hours at the office for the last part of the week and get Adrian to swim practice. Then, after the meet, she would have to break the news that she simply couldn't schedule it in anymore. But Adrian would have his memories of Daddy and the time they had spent together. And that was worth all the hassle.

Like all the other times she should be saying no to Adrian and Cole, she said, "Fine," and vowed to make it work for her son somehow.

Again, they high-fived as Isabella signed the required permission forms for the swimming competition.

Although she was beyond thrilled to see Adrian responding so well to Cole, nagging worry loomed. This would all be over as soon as Cole returned to New York.

"Headache?" Cole asked.

Isabella realized she'd been rubbing her temple. It was a gesture she was doing too often of late.

"Just rearranging my schedule in my mind for when you go back to New York."

Her days would be rushed. And they would be back to searching her father's medical journals for photos of Cole.

Isabella wasn't only worried for her son. She was worried for herself as well. She had been so foolish to fall for Cole a second time in a lifetime. Hadn't she learned her lesson the first time?

Grown-up Cole found his place in her heart just as easily as teenage Cole had fit there before. In fact, he was now a better fit, since he had wormed his way into his son's heart, too.

Cole looked as if he wanted to say something, maybe reassure her that everything would be all right. But in the end he had nothing to say.

Instead, he volunteered to do the dishes but Isabella declined. Adrian had so few hours left to spend with his daddy, she didn't want to take any away from him if she could help it.

Over the sound of the dishwasher's churning she strained to hear them together. When Cole read to Adrian, his deep voice melted her inside. It wasn't only the richness of his tone but the caring and concern that opened up all the places she'd closed off all those years ago.

They read the manga version of *Call of the Wild* twice through with nary a complaint from Cole about Adrian's request for a repeat performance. He seemed to accept Adrian's need for repetition as easily as he accepted Adrian's other quirks.

Swim practice had tired Adrian sufficiently to send him to bed without coercion—another improvement she could attribute to Cole. But, then, Adrian seemed to do whatever Daddy told him to do, instead of giving her that adolescent pushback that had started around his thirteenth birthday.

To avoid the tossing and turning of the night before,

Isabella decided to stay up until she couldn't keep her eyes open any longer.

"Would you like to watch television?" the hostess in her made her ask, although she yearned for a quieter evening.

"Only if you want to. I've got some reading to do."

"I'd rather read myself." She had a huge stack of trade magazines piled next to her favorite chair and never had time to read them. If only she could keep her concentration on the pages in front of her instead of the man so close and yet so out of reach.

"I'm going to make myself a cup of hot tea. Want one?"

"No, thanks."

As Isabella put the kettle on, she took her time observing Cole through the kitchen door. His glasses sat low on his nose as he frowned at a sheaf of documents. He made notes in the margins, chewing on his pen between comments.

In her mind's eye, she saw the same man as a boy fifteen years earlier as he'd pored over his history lesson, trying to narrow the gap between his inner-city grade-school education and the expensive, intense learning environment of St. Michael's. She couldn't have put a name to her admiration. At least, not to that aspect of her admiration. She could have readily told anyone she admired Cole's muscles, his brains, his sense of humor, and most of all she admired that he saw something hidden beneath her mousy exterior that he found both fascinating and sexy.

Now what did he see in her, beyond her son? Was there anything else to see?

As she settled in with her cup, Cole said, "Come and look at this."

As if it were a nightly occurrence, Bella sat next to him and tucked her feet under her. He handed her a report and held her tea as she read it.

"What am I looking at?"

"Ernest's vital signs before and after your therapy." Cole ran his finger under some data. I thought you might like to see the effects of your session."

How could she stop loving this man who understood how much it meant for her to know she made a difference? "I'm glad I could help."

"Ernest is scheduled for surgery tomorrow. He's terrified and asking for you. He wants you to observe the surgery. I know his request is unusual, but I told him I'd relay the message."

"Can I? Can you arrange for me to observe?"

"Yes, I can do that."

"Then, yes. Of course I will. Has he had any visitors at all?"

"Only the family whose daughter he saved, but they went back home days ago."

"How sad to have no one." If she was in the hospital, who would visit? David, for sure. He would bring Adrian as long as the problem wasn't too traumatic. Her father would find a way. Her colleagues would drop by. Would Cole come? "I can't imagine having no one to care about me."

"It can be rough." Sadness coated Cole's voice.

Other than his grandmother, had he been all alone as he'd grieved and recovered from his family's deaths?

"I'll stop by before I head to my office," she promised.

"Thanks." He took the report from her and handed back her tea. "With Ernest's surgery tomorrow afternoon, I may be running late getting home. Can you take care of Adrian's schedule?"

As she reached out, she couldn't resist touching him. The tingle went straight up her arm to her heart.

"I'll just go back to the way it was." That was what she would do with her whole life when he was gone. Go back to the way it had been.

"You're one of those, aren't you? One of those doctors whose care goes beyond the physical?"

"Of course. Why else practice medicine if not to make people feel better? And feeling better happens at a deeper lever than just the physical." He leaned close, so close she could feel that special prickle on her skin only he could produce. "That's why I find what you do so fascinating."

"You find my work fascinating?" she said stupidly, mesmerized by the spark in his eyes.

He moved in close and leaned down to whisper in her ear, "I find you fascinating."

Was this what she wanted? One more fling with Cole before he was gone from her life?

Before she could decide, he sat up straight, moving away from her. "I have other paperwork to show you."

As interesting as Bella found comparison charts, she didn't find them romantic and she had a strong suspicion that Cole didn't either. But they were the perfect excuse to put distance between them.

Cole had sensed—rather than seen—Bella pull back. He'd used all his willpower to play it casual but he wouldn't spoil this moment by asking for more than she could give.

Commitment.

The word popped into his head like an accusation.

There was more to life together than love.

Could he do it? Could he commit?

He had to admit that sitting in Isabella's den, with his feet propped on the hassock in front of him, and a beautiful woman who also happened to be the mother of his son within arm's reach, Cole had never felt more content in his entire life.

The simple exchange of plans, coordinating schedules to take care of Adrian, sharing a traditional family dinner, filled Cole's soul with wellness.

While he might never be a part of a traditional family again, the least he could do was provide for his son.

"I spent some time on the phone with my lawyers and accountants yesterday. I want to put my name on his birth certificate."

He detested that stillness Bella projected when she shut him out. Before she could protest, he held up a hand to hold off whatever response she was about to deliver. "No strings. I just want to give him whatever protection I can."

He could almost feel the thaw as Bella considered what he was offering.

"What kind of protection?"

"I'm a wealthy man, Bella." He couldn't hold back the pride in his voice when he confessed his success. "I can buy him whatever he needs. Being legally acknowledged as my son will make the legalese easier for all of us."

As if her thoughts drifted, her eyes went vague and her smile wistful. "Much of what he needs can't be bought."

"Am I right in thinking Adrian might never live on his own?"

"Not the way he is right now." Her shoulders bowed as if in defeat.

"I can make arrangements for his care past our lifetimes."

The brightness in her smile, the dampness in her eyes and the hope that radiated from her whole being gave purpose to all the work behind his financial success.

"You can do that, Cole? How to care for Adrian his whole lifetime has been my major worry since he was diagnosed."

"Yes, I can do that. I've already checked into several options. I'd like you to meet with my advisors and see what direction we want to head toward."

"Meet? In New Orleans?"

"It will be easier to fly you to New York than to fly a whole team of people to New Orleans."

"Adrian is afraid of airplanes."

"And so is his mother?" Cole guessed. How could some-one in this day and age be afraid to fly?

She gave him a sheepish grin. "They're big and noisy. How they stay up in the air defies reason to me."

"Then maybe it would be easier to bring them to you."

"Just like that?" She snapped her fingers. "You'll make ar-rangements for all these professionals to jaunt down to New Orleans for a couple of hours to lay out their plans for me?"

"Don't you get it, Bella? I'd do anything for my son." And for you.

"Again, thank you." She rose from her chair. "And now, before you start offering me the moon and the stars, I'm going to bed."

To bed. His mind filled with images of her naked, her head thrown back with all that glorious hair tumbling around her, shouting his name as she reached the peak of ecstasy.

If it could only be so once again.

He thought again of the ring he planned to offer her as soon as he could promise her a stable and secure future in New Orleans with it.

What would her answer be?

"I think I'll go for a walk. With Ernest's surgery tomor-row, I want to have a clear head. And thank you again for agreeing to observe the surgery. That will make all the dif-ference with his anxiety levels."

The walk didn't help. Neither did the cold shower.

He tried to think of the stars, of the moon, but all he could think of was Bella, looking at him like he'd hung the heav-ens just for her.

If only he could be that man…

Isabella stood before the guest bedroom door, raised her hand to knock, then put it down again.

The red silk of her new nightgown swirled around her thighs as she paced back and forth before his door.

This was it. Once she entered that room, there was no going back. As a fully grown woman knowing exactly what she was doing, she would be giving her heart to Cole, holding nothing back, and with no guarantee he would ever love her the way she loved him.

If she didn't knock, she would never know. She took a deep breath and squared her shoulders.

Cole. This was what she wanted. This was *who* she wanted.

And she was woman enough to go after her heart's desire. Three sharp, quick raps.

He opened his bedroom door and looked her up and down. "Bella?"

"Cole?" She echoed his tone.

"Say no." He growled it as if he issued a dare or a challenge.

"Yes." She pushed him backward into the room and closed the door behind them.

"You're sure?"

"Yes." She ran her finger around the waistband of his boxer shorts. "Yes, I'm sure."

"Show me."

Wanting to touch all of him at once, she ran her hand along his bare chest, letting her palms barely graze his sensitive nipples.

He sucked in air, a reaction that gave her all the confidence she needed to keep going.

As she ran her hands lower and lower, her own internal heat flamed hotter and hotter.

"You've got magic in those hands, lady." His voice was heavy and sultry.

"Watch what these hands can do." She tugged his shorts

down, feeling the strength and hardness of his muscles as she pushed the material lower and lower.

He stepped out of them then pulled her up to return the favor, brushing the straps of her nightgown off her shoulders, coasting his hands along her arms, circling each nipple with a long, strong finger until she ached for his touch.

His mouth followed his hands as he adored her with his kisses.

"I'm falling," she gasped. "Catch me."

In one move she was on the bed, looking up into Cole's eyes. Those eyes. How could eyes so dark flash like that?

"Fill me, Cole," she begged. "I ache for you."

"Here?" He ran a teasing finger across her most sensitive spot, making her squirm.

"Yes."

"Tell me what you want, Bella." He made quick work with the protection.

She barely gave him time to finish before she ran her fingernail down his chest. "I want you. All of you with nothing held back."

She arched toward him. "Do you want me?"

"More than I can say."

She traced a line down the length of him. "Then take me."

She was so ready for him. They fit together as if they were made for each other.

Isabella couldn't keep from moving, pulsing her hips into his. "Now, Cole. Now."

He met her stroke for stroke. Primal and intense, he rocked into her over and over again, bringing waves and waves of pleasure crashing through her.

She buried her head in his neck to stifle her screams as he let go of his own control and joined her in climax. His growl, escaping from deep down inside, seemed to spur her on and on until tears ran down her face.

Finally, lying side by side, they both gasped for air as their heartbeats fought for steadiness. Her face glowing with radiance, with pleasure, with pure female release, he had never seen anything as soul-stirring.

He kissed the dampness of her tears off her cheek, brushed her hair from her face, ran his fingertips down the silk of her arm and thought his heart would burst from the emotions expanding inside.

As they both caught their breaths, she laced her fingers in his, content to lie beside him, her silky smooth leg over his rough one. Her breath puffed in and out, a kitten snore that brought a smile to his face.

His mind drifted on a haze of bliss as all the tenseness left his body. Since time was meaningless, he had no idea how much later she asked, "How's your shoulder?" as she trickled her fingers over the places that usually ached.

"What shoulder?"

"Cole?"

"Hmm?" The concern in her voice cleared his head.

"I told Gloria."

"Told her what?"

"Told her you were Adrian's father. It will be all over the hospital tomorrow."

And he had thought his heart couldn't expand any further.

Barely above a whisper, she asked, "Are you okay with it?"

He swallowed to get the words past his thick throat. "I'm more than okay with it. I think this is the proudest moment of my life."

"There will be talk, and maybe questions."

"I imagine there will be. How would you like me to answer?"

"The truth."

"I can do that."

"Cole, if anyone says anything mean to you, let me know."

"And you'll beat them up for me?" The visual image he had of tiny Bella with boxing gloves squaring off to defend his honor made him laugh. "Thank you. Hopefully it won't come to blows in the back alley."

"I'll be sure to tell everyone that you didn't know."

"It doesn't matter what anyone else thinks, Bella. It never did. It's always been you who are important to me. Not them." He should say it. He should say he loved her.

But he couldn't get it out. The last time he'd said those words they'd been in bed, just like this, and he hadn't seen her again for fifteen years.

They were both older and hopefully wiser. But fear was irrational, whether it was fear of flying or fear of saying "I love you."

He would wait—wait until he could give her the assurances he hadn't been able to offer last time. Wait until he could tell her about the relocation and assure her that this time they would never be apart again.

She drifted to sleep cradled next to him and he followed soon after.

Sometime during the night she left him for her own bed.

It was the right thing to do because of Adrian but it still left a knot in his stomach.

The day couldn't come soon enough when the right thing to do would be to stay.

CHAPTER THIRTEEN

THE first thought on Bella's mind on awakening was that she hadn't told him.

How could she have fallen asleep without telling Cole she loved him?

But, then, he hadn't told her either. They had both fallen asleep too soon.

The house was eerily quiet around her and the sun was too bright in her window. How late had she slept?

How long had it been since she'd felt this rested?

Her clock showed her half the morning was gone. Rearranging her schedule to observe Ernest's surgery had given her a free morning, but she hadn't intended to spend it in bed.

But she still had time for a nice long bath and to fix herself a leisurely breakfast—although she had gotten spoiled by Cole's breakfasts already.

She would tell him tonight, no matter how late he might be.

Isabella grinned to herself. She would tell him in bed tonight, as she had intended to tell him last night.

Communication. They would talk. No matter how much comfort she found in living for the moment, she would make plans for the future, a future with Cole.

She had intended to say hello to Cole before he went into surgery, but she'd had to spend some time talking Ernest through his panic before he was wheeled to surgery and she missed him.

Instead, she took her place in the gallery, fully intending to avert her gaze for most of the procedure. But she knew the moment Cole walked into the O.R. The pull was as strong as if he had called out her name.

While she couldn't see his mouth behind the mask, she saw the smile in his eyes. She was sure she had a broad enough smile for both of them.

As he walked into the room, the patient on the table took most of his focus, but the woman in the gallery above him still pulled his attention. He looked up to see her looking down.

Seeing Bella, knowing she was seeing him at his best, gave Cole a sense of pride he had searched for all his life.

Instead of distracting him, she made him sharper, more aware, more in tune with everyone and everything around him.

Cole always felt a strange buzz in surgery, a kind of energy that seemed to race through his body, swirl around the patient and fill the sterile field.

Today, as he scrubbed in as consultant to Dr. Lockhart, he relished that electric feel. The only other time he'd ever felt this way had been with Bella, only that was so much deeper, so much more intimate than this.

He loved her. He had always loved her, never stopped loving her. But now he loved as a man, where before he'd loved as a boy. It seemed to be a broader, deeper, more encompassing kind of love.

"Ready, Doctor?" Dr. Lockhart asked beside him.

Cole took a cleansing breath to get his head back into the game. "Ready."

Then Cole took a good look at the patient's shoulder

prepped for surgery and his whole world centered on the task before him.

They had expected a textbook case of a glenoid labrum tear. But once in, the surgery quickly became complicated by posterior neuroma-in-continuity extending into the auxiliary nerve.

The microsurgery was tedious and delicate, more of an urging of nerve stimulation and conservative serial sectioning than a cut-and-stitch kind of job. Dr. Lockhart was fastidious and light-handed as well as innovative, qualities that would make him the perfect practice partner.

Ernest was fortunate to have such a skilled surgeon operating. And Cole could now see why the sports clinic was asking such high buy-ins. The costs were worth it to have both Dr. Lockhart and Dr. Wong in partnership.

Three hours in and Cole's neck and shoulder were screaming under the tension. Any amount of shifting and shrugging did nothing to relieve the pain.

"Can you help me out here, Dr. Lassiter?" Dr. Lockhart asked, pointing with his scalpel.

"Forceps," Cole ordered, holding out his hand and waiting for the snap.

The team of surgical nurses assembled was the best he'd ever worked with. The instrument came quick and clean.

He closed his fingers—milliseconds too slowly. And the forceps fell into the field, clinking on the table on the way down to the floor.

Over the mask, Dr. Lockhart raised his eyes in question.

Cole knew the answer. It hit him in the pit of his stomach.

Surgery. The one thing he was born to do was in jeopardy.

From the gallery he felt Isabella's eyes on him. She had witnessed his downfall.

"Forceps," he immediately called again.

The nurse supplied him with another pair, hesitating a second before turning them loose this time. The clumsy handoff felt like his first few years of training.

He kept his hand steady by nothing but sheer willpower.

Once he was no longer needed and he could release his hold, his brow was sweating as though he'd just performed the procedure himself.

Dr. Lockhart liked to close himself, something Cole always did, too. At the last suture he pronounced the procedure "Done."

As he exited the operating room, he whispered to Cole, "I'll see you in my office this afternoon. I'll have my staff discreetly schedule radiology appointments as well."

It wasn't a suggestion, or even a kind offer. It was a surgeon taking care of his profession as a whole. Dr. Lockhart would examine Cole and make the decision he had to make, for the good of all.

Instead of finding herself queasy, she had found herself fascinated with everything about the surgical procedure.

Knowing her father had been an early pioneer in the area, knowing he had saved lives as well as given back the mobility that gave a purpose to so many people's lives, raised her respect for her father in a whole new way.

Seeing Cole in such a heroic role made her heart pound for him.

She could see the intensity of his eyes above his surgical mask as he discussed the case with Dr. Lockhart. Even with the sound muted in the observation gallery, she could tell each man had the utmost respect for the other's opinion.

He held out his hand for an instrument.

Then it fell from his hand. If she hadn't been watching so carefully, she would have missed the bleak expression in his eyes.

For a split second Dr. Lockhart raised his focus from his

patient and centered it on Cole instead, looking concerned, worried and sad.

Isabella didn't quite understand what had just happened, but she knew in the pit of her stomach it wasn't good.

Cole had said he might be late.

She waited for Cole as long as she could but she had to pick up Adrian. She wanted to sooth that anguish she had seen. Maybe there was paperwork, or post-surgery examination.

Maybe he would join them at swim practice or at dinner.

But she had a bad feeling, a feeling that wouldn't go away no matter how she tried to rationalize it.

What she had seen in Cole's eyes when he'd looked at her in the gallery had been goodbye.

In Dr. Lockhart's private office Cole didn't need to be a radiologist to interpret the images on the four oversize computer monitors.

"I'm a shoulder man, and your problem is in your spine. You need a few more opinions. But what I think I see is degenerative disk disease with spinal stenosis in the cervical spine. I'm sorry, Cole." Dr. Lockhart pointed to the brachial plexus. "See the impingement? This is causing your paresthesia as well as the pain and numbness. We can give you anti-inflammatories and the occasional spinal injection to ease the symptoms."

"Surgery?"

"We could try an anterior cervical disk fusion but ACDFs haven't proved very successful for stopping the pain or the deterioration.

"Or the numbness?"

"Or the numbness," Dr. Lockhart confirmed. "You'll want to consult with several spinal specialists before you decide for surgery."

"What caused it?"

Dr. Lockhart pointed to the deterioration. "Degenerative disk disease can be inherited. Did anyone in your family have this problem? Or have you had an old injury in this area?"

"I had an injury when I was twelve. That time is fairly fuzzy, though, and I don't remember what the diagnosis was." He reached to rub his neck, then put his hand back down again.

To combat memories of that cold, dark night, Cole deliberately thought of Bella, thought of how she'd looked last night as she'd slept in his arms.

Real-time physical pain moved out of the spotlight as remembrances of physical pleasure with Bella moved into it and he could breathe again.

"I don't know about family history. Both my parents died when they were about my age."

"I'm sorry. I didn't know. I'm sure they would be very proud of their son with all your accomplishments."

"My past accomplishments."

"There are plenty of career paths a brilliant physician like you could follow besides surgery." Dr. Lockhart paused, trying to find the right thing to say. "I'm sorry, Cole."

Dr. Lockhart's tone was the same as he would use at a funeral to express his sympathy.

His sentiment was appropriate. The diagnosis meant the professional death of a surgeon. Cole would have to be reborn in a role that didn't include the one skill in his life that made him special.

Dr. Lockhart clicked off the images. "I'm afraid the partners will have to be informed. I can try to keep it quiet for a few days if you want to get those other opinions first, but you'll need to hurry. You know how gossip spreads in this place."

Not only did his diagnosis put his career in danger, it also endangered his fiscal soundness, which endangered his financial care of Adrian and Bella.

Cole stared at the monitors, seeing a future as stark as the black-and-white images displayed there.

CHAPTER FOURTEEN

HE HAD to think about Bella and Adrian. He had to think—but all he could do was feel. Despair had him driving slowly back to Bella's home in a fog.

Who was he now? All he'd ever wanted to be was a surgeon and now his whole identity was in jeopardy.

Cole longed for Bella and the comfort she could give him. But what could he give her in return? Even the financial security he'd promised her and their son was at risk.

Get a second opinion, Dr. Lockhart had suggested—no, had insisted on. And Cole had access to the best spinal specialists on the planet.

What did he have to offer Bella?

He didn't know. And he wouldn't burden her until he found some answers. Between her father and her son, she had enough people to care for, without adding him into the mix.

He scribbled a note and stuffed it in an envelope he'd picked up at the hotel: "Have gone to New York for testing. Will call you later with details."

With one hand he shoveled clothes into his suitcase and with the other he punched speed dial for the airlines. As he listened to the flights available he checked his watch and jotted down airlines and flight times.

If traffic was light, if seats were available, if all the stars were aligned, he could make the flight to New York tonight.

Using his phone, he punched buttons until he'd purchased his ticket then left for the airport at a run. He needed to catch that flight.

If he arrived early enough, he could call in favors and arrange appointments and diagnostic tests for tomorrow.

Traffic was kind, but airport security was not.

Airport security made a big issue out of the ring in his pocket and he almost missed his flight.

As he sat in first class, waiting for the plane to take off, he took out the ring that had kept him from leaving New Orleans, turning it to create refracted light rainbows on his empty water glass.

Between being scanned, shuffled, queued up, ordered to buckle up as they had to leave the gate immediately to avoid the impending thunderstorm coming their way and taking off, he didn't even have a chance to turn his phone back on.

But he had no idea what he would have said, anyway.

Once seated, he had too much time to think about the woman he'd bought the ring for.

He had picked out the ring that morning right after he'd dropped Adrian at school. He had intended to promise a secure future in the city she had taught him to call home again.

Instead, he would be sitting in his sterile apartment, staring at the bright city lights of New York.

He'd done the same thing over fifteen years ago.

He'd come so close to asking her to marry him last night— so close. Had he known instinctively to hold off?

The last thing Bella needed was another person in her life to take care of.

What would she think of damaged goods? He gave her more credit than to kick him to the curb, but how could she help but look at him differently now? He certainly saw himself differently.

No, worse than that. He didn't see himself at all. Right now he was a purposeless man.

Cole rubbed his neck and shoulder, feeling the ache all the way through to his heart.

Bella had been calling Cole all day. She called him between clients, and as she waited for Adrian at the speech therapist, and now as he finished up swim practice. As Adrian buckled up to head home, Bella called Cole once more, listened to his voicemail and hung up.

Why did this feel just like fifteen years ago when she had called and called in vain?

As she drove into her driveway, her house felt empty. She knew he was gone before she even checked his closet or picked up the note on his bedside table.

An old but too familiar fear began to fill her.

No. This would not be like last time.

Bella stared at the envelope in her hand as the cryptic numbers began to make sense.

"Come on, Adrian. We're going to take a ride on an airplane."

Grabbing the manga book and wolf, she rushed her son to the car.

As she swerved in and out of traffic, all her thoughts were wrapped around Cole. Didn't he know he could come to her for comfort? Didn't he know she wanted to be strong for him?

No. He didn't know any of those things. He'd never been loved before when he'd needed it most.

Would it have made a difference if she had told him she loved him last night? Somehow she didn't think so.

As she pulled into a parking space at the airport and began the three-mile hike to the terminal, she couldn't decide if she would strangle Cole or hug him when she finally caught up with him.

One thing was for sure, she would tell him a thing or two and when she got done talking, he would have no doubt about how she felt.

Bella had to laugh at her own hypocrisy. How could Cole know how she felt? She had never told him. Why did it take almost losing him again for her to finally be courageous enough to speak her mind?

As she ran to the ticket booth, she saw the flight Cole had circled on the envelope had already departed.

"Two tickets to New York on the next flight out."

"Yes, ma'am. Baggage?"

"No baggage." *If only that was true in every sense of the word.*

She handed over her credit card to the attendant. Buying tickets for two at the last minute would cost more than she made in a month, but Cole would be paying off the balance.

Only for Cole would Bella risk her life and that of her child by getting on an airplane. Her experience in hiding her emotions came in handy as they took off and Bella carved grooves into the armrests with her fingernails. Amazingly, the plane stayed up in the air the whole trip.

And Bella was wrong. Her son loved to fly—as long as she read to him. By the time they touched down in New York, Adrian was one happy boy on his way to see his daddy.

Unlike the passengers who'd had to listen to the manga version of *Call of the Wild* forty-seven times without a break.

When the taxi drive dropped them off at Cole's high-rise apartment building, Isabella gave her last two twenty-dollar bills to the taxi driver. He sped away without giving her change.

With her cash gone and credit cards now totally maxed out, there truly was no going back.

Bella realized this was the first leap of faith she had ever taken, and it felt terrifying yet exhilarating.

She pounded on the door to Cole's New York apartment, ignoring the eagle eyes she received from his neighbor. She was determined to stay until she got her answers. This would not be like the last time, full of misunderstandings and lost love.

No, this time she would have her say before she let him walk away.

If he thought he could come back into her life, make her fall in love with him and then just walk away, he had a thing or two left to learn about her.

When the door handle turned, she couldn't step back fast enough to keep from falling forward. He caught her against his chest. The fresh smell of soap and Cole, the feel of his warm body against hers, the special electricity that flowed from his body to hers filled her senses. No, she was not going to meekly let this go.

"Bella, you're here? You flew? What are you doing here?"

"I've found there is one thing I'm more afraid of than airplanes and that's letting things go unspoken between us again." She should stand on her own two feet right now, but Cole didn't seem to be too quick to let her go. Not that she was pushing away from him.

"This isn't going to be like last time." She finally found the willpower. Putting her hands on his chest, she took a step back.

She pulled out the stark white envelope from her purse, slapping it against her opposite hand. "A letter isn't going to be enough for me—not this time."

Holding up the envelope, she said, very distinctly, "Whatever you have to say to me, say it to my face." As she tore through the thick paper, she felt like she was tearing through her heart.

"Why, Cole?" She looked up at him, ignoring the tears welling in her eyes. "Why?"

Cole watched the pieces scatter around them. "My shoulder—it may be something serious. I may not be a surgeon anymore."

"I'm not looking for the perfect man. Perfection is impossible." She held both his hands in hers. "Cole Lassiter, I love you, flaws and all."

"And I love you, Bella Allante, with all my heart."

"And our son?"

"And our son, more than life itself." He looked into her eyes. "I may not have a position in New Orleans, not if the spinal specialist can't fix me up."

"I want to be with you, Cole, here in New York, or wherever else you may end up."

"Even if I have to leave the medical profession?"

"You are more than a surgeon, Cole Lassiter. You're Adrian's father. You understand him better than anyone else in his life. And you understand me. You're the man who makes me feel whole. You're my soul mate, and I am yours." She laid her hand along his cheek. "We were always meant to be together."

"Together, forever." Cole dug into his pocket and pulled out a ring, small and delicate. "Bella, will you marry me?"

"Yes, I'll marry you. And we will never be apart again."

As Cole wrapped her in his arms, she whispered in his ear, "I was wrong about perfection being impossible. We're the perfect family, flaws and all."

* * * * *

Mills & Boon® Hardback

August 2012

ROMANCE

Contract with Consequences	Miranda Lee
The Sheikh's Last Gamble	Trish Morey
The Man She Shouldn't Crave	Lucy Ellis
The Girl He'd Overlooked	Cathy Williams
A Tainted Beauty	Sharon Kendrick
One Night With The Enemy	Abby Green
The Dangerous Jacob Wilde	Sandra Marton
His Last Chance at Redemption	Michelle Conder
The Hidden Heart of Rico Rossi	Kate Hardy
Marrying the Enemy	Nicola Marsh
Mr Right, Next Door!	Barbara Wallace
The Cowboy Comes Home	Patricia Thayer
The Rancher's Housekeeper	Rebecca Winters
Her Outback Rescuer	Marion Lennox
Monsoon Wedding Fever	Shoma Narayanan
If the Ring Fits...	Jackie Braun
Sydney Harbour Hospital: Ava's Re-Awakening	Carol Marinelli
How To Mend A Broken Heart	Amy Andrews

MEDICAL

Falling for Dr Fearless	Lucy Clark
The Nurse He Shouldn't Notice	Susan Carlisle
Every Boy's Dream Dad	Sue MacKay
Return of the Rebel Surgeon	Connie Cox

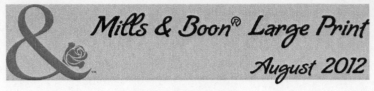

Mills & Boon® Large Print

August 2012

ROMANCE

A Deal at the Altar	Lynne Graham
Return of the Moralis Wife	Jacqueline Baird
Gianni's Pride	Kim Lawrence
Undone by His Touch	Annie West
The Cattle King's Bride	Margaret Way
New York's Finest Rebel	Trish Wylie
The Man Who Saw Her Beauty	Michelle Douglas
The Last Real Cowboy	Donna Alward
The Legend of de Marco	Abby Green
Stepping out of the Shadows	Robyn Donald
Deserving of His Diamonds?	Melanie Milburne

HISTORICAL

The Scandalous Lord Lanchester	Anne Herries
Highland Rogue, London Miss	Margaret Moore
His Compromised Countess	Deborah Hale
The Dragon and the Pearl	Jeannie Lin
Destitute On His Doorstep	Helen Dickson

MEDICAL

Sydney Harbour Hospital: Lily's Scandal	Marion Lennox
Sydney Harbour Hospital: Zoe's Baby	Alison Roberts
Gina's Little Secret	Jennifer Taylor
Taming the Lone Doc's Heart	Lucy Clark
The Runaway Nurse	Dianne Drake
The Baby Who Saved Dr Cynical	Connie Cox

Mills & Boon® Hardback

September 2012

ROMANCE

Unlocking her Innocence	Lynne Graham
Santiago's Command	Kim Lawrence
His Reputation Precedes Him	Carole Mortimer
The Price of Retribution	Sara Craven
Just One Last Night	Helen Brooks
The Greek's Acquisition	Chantelle Shaw
The Husband She Never Knew	Kate Hewitt
When Only Diamonds Will Do	Lindsay Armstrong
The Couple Behind the Headlines	Lucy King
The Best Mistake of Her Life	Aimee Carson
The Valtieri Baby	Caroline Anderson
Slow Dance with the Sheriff	Nikki Logan
Bella's Impossible Boss	Michelle Douglas
The Tycoon's Secret Daughter	Susan Meier
She's So Over Him	Joss Wood
Return of the Last McKenna	Shirley Jump
Once a Playboy…	Kate Hardy
Challenging the Nurse's Rules	Janice Lynn

MEDICAL

Her Motherhood Wish	Anne Fraser
A Bond Between Strangers	Scarlet Wilson
The Sheikh and the Surrogate Mum	Meredith Webber
Tamed by her Brooding Boss	Joanna Neil

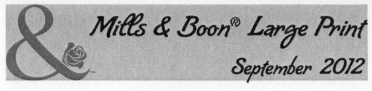

Mills & Boon® Large Print

September 2012

ROMANCE

HISTORICAL

MEDICAL